A Candlelight Ecstasy Romance™

A CANDLELIGHT ECSTASY ROMANCE™

HIS KISS WENT THROUGH HER LIKE FIRE. . . .

She had no will to resist him, and in truth, it never entered her mind. In one brief instant this man swept aside her every inhibition.

Elisa's name came from his lips over and over again until she finally understood that she was not the only one who had lost control.

"God, this is crazy," Garth grated through his teeth. "You're just a kid."

"I'm not a kid!" she insisted, daring at last to meet his skeptical gaze. "I am a woman."

"Are you woman enough to understand what I want?"

NEVER AS STRANGERS

Suzanne Simmons

A CANDLELIGHT ECSTASY ROMANCE™

Published by
Dell Publishing Co., Inc.
1 Dag Hammarskjold Plaza
New York, New York 10017

Dell ®-TM 681510, Dell Publishing Co., Inc.

Candlelight Ecstasy Romance™ is a trademark of
Dell Publishing Co., Inc., New York, New York.

ISBN: 0–440–16278–5

Printed in the United States of America

First printing—March 1982

Dear Reader:

In response to your continued enthusiasm for Candlelight Ecstasy Romances™, we are increasing the number of new titles from four to six per month.

We are delighted to present sensuous novels set in America, depicting modern American men and women as they confront the provocative problems of modern relationships.

Throughout the history of the Candlelight line, Dell has tried to maintain a high standard of excellence to give you the finest in reading enjoyment. That is and will remain our most ardent ambition.

Anne Gisonny
Editor
Candlelight Romances

NEVER AS STRANGERS

Dedicated to my son, Steve.

CHAPTER ONE

The young woman stood up and stretched, looking very much like a tabby in her black- and tan-striped robe, strands of loose brown hair tucked behind her ears. She arched her spine, rubbing the back of her neck as she dropped the pair of reading glasses on the open book beside her carefully scribbled notes. God, she was tired! She needed a much deserved break. Besides, she was suddenly hungry.

In an almost caressing motion Elisa Harrington reached out a hand and ran it along the well-polished surface of the desk. Memories rushed in, further softening the features already in repose. Only the scarcely discernible twist to the generous mouth betrayed the pain that even now accompanied those memories of another time and place.

It had been Carl Harrington's desk, and as long as Elisa could remember, it held the coveted position in her father's study while he was alive. Overly large and certainly not a thing of beauty, it had always been crammed with scraps of paper, presumably invaluable notes on *Richard III* or *King Lear,* and stacked high with an assortment of books, as cluttered as the room around it. Elisa still found it curious that her father had been able to find anything at all under the circumstances. Organized clutter was definitely not her style. Her own room at the boardinghouse was neat to the point of being Spartan—as was her life.

After Carl Harrington's death Elisa had refused to part with his desk. It was one of the few pieces she and Amanda had chosen not to sell at auction. It had occupied one wall of this otherwise elegant bedroom for the past eight years, strangely at odds with the luxury that surrounded it. Perhaps it was time, after all, to have it moved to her own apartment. She would tell Amanda this weekend.

With a flick of her wrist Elisa snapped the psychology book closed. Hardly the kind of text that had adorned the desk in her father's day. For Carl Harrington had been a well-respected man and a Shakespearean scholar of some merit. Always a little vague, of another world and another time, he had been more at home with the Elizabethan age than his own. A man who could deal ruthlessly with the lofty question of good and evil, while utterly hopeless when it came to the mundane, the everyday. He had been devastated by the death of his pretty young wife in a freak automobile accident. Elisa had been a nine-year-old child at the time. Her own memories of the lovely and deceptively ethereal creature who had been her anchor to the real world as well as her mother were filled with the sound of her voice and the haunting scent of Chanel No. 5.

The young woman wondered even yet if her father had married Amanda more for the sake of convenience than for any great love on his part. He was hardly the man to deal with a young daughter on the brink of puberty. But whatever the reason or reasons it was Amanda who had been there to guide Elisa through the throes of adolescence, who had lent a sympathetic ear to the outpourings of a besotted teen-ager imagining herself in love for the first time. And it was Amanda who had stood by her when the world crumbled into ashes about her feet at the untimely death of her father. Elisa would always be grateful to her stepmother for those times and so many more. There was a bond of tensile strength between them that had withstood even the test of Amanda's remarriage.

Elisa admitted she had been disconcerted when her stepmother married James Rollins barely a year after Carl Harrington's death. It was primarily out of respect for her feelings that Amanda had not married him sooner. Yet even at sixteen she had recognized that her stepmother was still a young woman and was perhaps at last loved for herself.

Yes, Elisa nodded her head emphatically as she looked about the beautifully decorated bedroom, she understood Amanda's reasons for becoming Mrs. James Rollins. Besides being an attractive man who was obviously in love with his second wife, James Rollins was a successful businessman who represented not only financial security but a position in the community as well.

That kind of thing mattered little to Elisa—not that she blamed her stepmother for wanting more out of life than to eke by as the widow of a university professor. They had not been difficult years really, the four Elisa had spent in this house. She supposed she might even have become quite fond of James given the chance. But the poor man had had his hands full smoothing the way for his new wife with the willful, then eleven-year-old Charlotte, let alone trying the same for a teen-ager he scarcely knew himself.

It had been perfectly clear from the beginning that Charlotte had no intentions of allowing Elisa to usurp her own place in the household. Oh, she had tried her best to make life miserable for Elisa, and it was only by the most determined of efforts that she had not been allowed to succeed.

At first it was Charlotte's compulsive need for Amanda's and James's undivided attention that had driven the younger child to jealous fits of temper. Later it was the

13

young men who came to the house to see Elisa. After losing the interest of one too many young men to the precocious fifteen-year-old, Elisa had stopped bringing her friends home. She simply arranged to meet them elsewhere. When she was twenty, she moved out of the Rollins house altogether, coming back only for an occasional weekend. It was the one thing she had done that earned Charlotte's total approval.

Now Charlotte was twenty herself. Tall and sophisticated, strikingly blond and beautiful, she was seemingly all that Elisa was not. Yet this somehow failed to evoke any envy in the older girl. Charlotte managed to be civil to Elisa, if a bit condescending. Her attitude did not provoke anger or resentment, but rather pity—pity Elisa was wise enough to conceal, knowing instinctively it was the last thing on earth Charlotte Rollins would want from her.

The differences between the two young women, separated by far more than just five years in age, were starkly evident in the surroundings in which each had grown up. Miss Charlotte in the sprawling French provincial house in an affluent section of Madison, Elisa Harrington in the happily cluttered cottage near the university campus, knowing more of Shakespeare's light and dark comedies by ten than most of her father's students. They simply did not speak the same language, she and Charlotte. They never had.

Enough of that! With an impish grin that defied her nearly twenty-five years the young woman dismissed the unpleasant subject of Charlotte Rollins from her mind. She swept down the stairs, driven by a ravenous hunger that demanded to be satisfied.

"Now, Millie, my dear, where did you hide the chicken salad?" muttered Elisa as she opened the refrigerator door and began to rummage through its contents. "Ah, there you are!" she chortled, reaching for the container. With the mayonnaise and chicken salad in one hand and a

14

carton of milk in the other, she elbowed the door closed behind her.

She was talking to herself again. And why not? Elisa thought as she poured herself a large glass of cold milk. She was all alone in the vast house, Mrs. Lawrence, affectionately known as Millie, having retired to her own apartment; Amanda and James out for the evening; and Charlotte—who knew where Charlotte was?

Elisa supposed she was out with Garth Brandau, the man of the moment. Charlotte had been seeing him for the past several months, though it was odd she could not recall Charlotte mentioning she had a date with him this evening. Oh, well, the young blonde had numerous friends, and Elisa was hardly in the habit of keeping tabs on her. She was privy to James Rollins's hope that a formal announcement might come about between the well-known architect and his daughter. Garth Brandau was considered a perfect match for Charlotte despite a difference of fifteen years in their ages. He was handsome, talented, and eligible—very eligible—and came from a moneyed family.

Yes, doubtlessly Charlotte was out with the eminently suitable Garth Brandau. Elisa wondered if the man had any idea what the Rollins father and daughter had in mind for him. But then, he was old enough to take care of himself, she reflected with a wry smile. She had her own future to consider and no one man played the leading role in her plans. Not Professor Hartman, who had made it clear he would not be averse to having an affair with her. And not Chuck Stephenson—dear, sweet, impractical Chuck, who actually believed that two mouths could eat as cheaply as one.

Elisa's plans did include sharing an apartment with a friend while she continued to work at the university library and attend classes. She had nearly completed the hours required for her master's degree, relying on a small

15

annuity from her father and what money she could earn herself. She had politely but firmly refused any offer of financial assistance from James Rollins, determined to make it on her own.

Elisa was leaning against the kitchen counter, absently sipping her milk between bites of chicken salad, when a length of soft gray fur wound itself around her bare legs, purring its arrival.

"It's a darn good thing no one is here but me, Ophelia," the young woman scolded, putting the sandwich down in order to gather the cat up into her arms. "You know you're not allowed beyond the back porch. Millie would have kittens if she caught you in her kitchen." Elisa buried her face in the silky coat, trailing her cheek along the feline's neck. "I've missed you, poor old puss. I know I haven't been back to see you in weeks and weeks, but I've been busy studying. I'm sorry. Will you forgive me if I share my milk with you?"

With Ophelia tucked beneath one arm, Elisa placed a small bowl on the kitchen floor and poured a little of the milk from her glass into the dish.

"Better enjoy your few brief moments of freedom, my sweet. Soon enough you must return to a life of exile." At the jangling of the front doorbell Elisa straightened up like a shot. "Now, who do you suppose that could be?" she asked her furry companion. "You'd better go. It just might be Charlotte. She has been known to forget her key on more than one occasion."

With a quick "Shoo-shoo" to the cat, Elisa sped down the hall to the rather imposing front entranceway, remembering at the last moment to peer through the security view with one squinted eye. She was taken aback to see none other than Garth Brandau standing on the other side.

She drew back the lock and opened the door, self-consciously clutching at the lapels of her bathrobe separated

16

in the playful scuffle with Ophelia. Elisa stood there, one hand at her throat, staring up into the man's face. The play of shadows across the handsome features lent them a sinister air. She shook her head as if to dispel the illusion, finally finding her voice.

"Oh, Mr. Brandau." There was a noted lack of enthusiasm.

He looked faintly amused. "Hello, Elisa."

"I . . . we weren't expecting anyone at this time of night. The doorbell startled me." It was rather plainly an accusation.

"Sorry."

"I'm afraid Charlotte isn't here. Though I'm quite sure she wouldn't have gone out if she'd had any idea you were dropping by." Could he discern the facetiousness in her voice? Elisa doubted it.

"It's all right, I didn't let her know. And please . . . Garth," he said in a commanding voice.

Elisa was genuinely puzzled for a moment. "Garth?" she repeated dumbly.

The man suddenly thrust his head forward. "May I come in?"

"Y-yes, of course." The young woman recovered and stepped back. "I'm sorry Amanda and James aren't here either. They went to some kind of political reception. I honestly don't know when any of them will be back."

"There's no need to apologize, you know. I decided to stop on the spur of the moment." A hint of impatience crept into his resonant baritone. "I suppose you were studying," the man added as an afterthought.

"Yes, yes, I was." Elisa was surprised Garth Brandau even remembered she was a student.

"It looks as though you were taking a break. Mind if I join you?"

"But how did you know?" she asked, feeling rather foolish.

17

Her question was answered with a look and a single word as he reached out to trace the line along her lips. "Milk."

The man smiled down at her then. Elisa felt herself shiver at the touch of his hand on her skin, understanding instantly the attraction Garth Brandau held for a woman and for the first time perhaps even envying Charlotte just a little. She had met a few men who seemed to possess this kind of charisma. She neither trusted them nor liked them, but there was something about them . . .

The young woman ran her tongue quickly along her upper lip in an attempt to erase the telltale evidence. "Would you like something to drink?" she finally offered.

Garth chuckled appreciatively at some private joke. "I wouldn't dream of interrupting a late-night raid on the refrigerator. I'll just have whatever you're having."

"You want milk and chicken salad?" Elisa heard the disbelief in her own voice.

"I happen to be quite fond of chicken salad."

"Would you like to go into the living room while I get your sandwich and milk, then?"

"You were in the kitchen, weren't you?"

Elisa turned back to answer him and ran smack dab into a wall of bone and hard muscle. "Well, yes, but—" She nervously took a step away from him.

"Then, the kitchen it is," Garth said, cutting her short.

"I'll bet Charlotte never entertained you in the scullery." Elisa laughed lightly under her breath as she led the way toward the back of the house. She bit down on her lip, realizing it had sounded rather catty. She hadn't meant it that way. Or had she? To disguise her discomfort she busied herself at the counter, firing questions at the man while she went to work. "Do you prefer wheat, rye, or white bread? Mayonnaise? Lettuce?"

"Rye, yes, and yes, please," Garth responded, as he

watched the girl go about the business of making him a sandwich with practiced efficiency.

"Would you like to sit down?" Elisa motioned toward a table in the corner.

"Thank you, but I would prefer to stand." The young brunette shrugged her shoulders expressively, as if to say he could suit himself. "I've been chained to a drafting board all day," the man said by way of explanation, leaning an elbow on the counter beside her.

"You do look haggard," Elisa said in her usual straight-forward manner. If Garth Brandau was offended, he didn't show it. It occurred to her that here was a man no doubt accustomed to honey dripping from a woman's lips. Well, she'd be damned if she would allow herself to fall into that cliché. One could be honest and still polite.

Garth looked at her with a studied gaze, as though seeing her for the first time. And it was indeed the first time they had been alone.

"You know, you look like a kid in that getup. How many years are there between you and Charlotte anyway?"

"I take it she hasn't told you much about us—me." Elisa met his inquiring gaze.

"Not much." The man stopped to take a long gulp of milk. "I know you're a student."

"A graduate student, Mr. Brandau." She was suddenly determined to set him straight on a few points. "Hasn't Charlotte told you I'm five years older than she is?" In truth, her birthday was still several weeks away, but she saw no reason to mention it.

"You could have fooled me," he said, his eyes glinting curiously. "You and Charlotte are remarkably . . . different." The man seemed hesitant to put a name to it.

"We're as different as night and day is what you mean. And why shouldn't we be? Surely Charlotte has told you that we aren't related. Yes, I see she did tell you that

19

much." Elisa read something there in his face he had not meant for her to see. Garth started to make some sign of protest. "No, it's all right. Believe me, I'm well aware there is no love lost between Charlotte and me. We only met a handful of times before my stepmother married James Rollins. Two only children thrown together. Amanda and James tried, but it was a difficult situation at best."

"That does explain a lot," Garth observed as he took a bite of his sandwich. "This is really very good. Thanks. Aren't you going to join me?" He indicated the plate she had left behind to answer the doorbell.

"I'd almost forgotten," the girl mumbled, reaching for her own sandwich. After a moment or two she continued. "I heard Charlotte mention at dinner that you were working on some big project." She swallowed and waited, not knowing quite what to say to this man, feeling ill at ease eating while his observant eyes seemed to take in her slightest move.

"Yes, I can imagine how Charlotte 'mentioned' it too." His lips tightened into a narrow line. "She doesn't seem to understand that I can't always be at her beck and call. Dammit, my work necessarily takes a great deal of my time and attention!" Garth clamped his mouth shut, as though he may have said more than he intended. Indiscretion was hardly his style.

Elisa felt herself grow warm under his scrutiny. For Charlotte, with a childish pout on her perfectly made-up mouth, had indeed complained that Garth was ignoring her because of some "stupid" project. Evidently he was astute enough to have guessed her reaction. But what did the man expect if he was going to go around dating a girl scarcely out of her teens?

"Do you enjoy being an architect? Or is that rather a naive question?" Elisa faced him, smiling tentatively, but quite serious.

"Not at all. Yes, I do enjoy being an architect. If I didn't, I wouldn't do it," he stated, smiling back at her.

Elisa believed him. She also believed that Garth Brandau was a man who would not waste even one moment doing something he did not want to do. Under the guise of listening the young woman studied him, seeing a man of above-average height, though not exceedingly tall, perhaps nearing six feet in shoes. His brown hair was thick and prematurely flecked with gray. The handsome face was marked by a neat mustache and what Elisa would tongue-in-cheek term "bedroom eyes"—deep green eyes that frequently seemed focused on something in the distance as he spoke. There was a little bit of the dreamer about Garth Brandau. Not that he was soft. No, indeed. If anything, the man appeared to be chiseled out of stone, his muscular athlete's body supporting the rumor that he played as hard as he worked. He had the reputation of being a brilliant architect with a penchant for getting his own way. If he had an Achilles' heel, no one knew what it was.

Elisa blinked and leaned back against the kitchen counter, listening attentively as he talked.

"I've just completed the preliminary drawings for a government housing development. It's been kind of a pet project of mine for the past couple of months. Too many architects work only for clients who can afford custom-designed homes and buildings. I do some myself, but there is a real need for the profession to concern itself with all levels of housing. We must have good architects designing low-cost units. It's a challenge to come up with a good design at the most reasonable price tag possible. God knows there are enough blights in our cities as it is." His voice rang with conviction. "Charlotte accuses me of sounding like a fire-and-brimstone preacher on the subject. I guess I do sometimes," Garth said, half laughing and half angry. "This particular project has taken a lot of my time the past couple of weeks. I stopped by to tell Charlotte it was finished, that I would have more time to spend with her now."

"I'm sure she'll be delighted to hear that," Elisa murmured without sarcasm.

"No doubt she will," he echoed absently, as though his mind were on something else. After a moment or two he came back to her with a wrenching effort. Garth stared at her fixedly, his eyes piercing, no faraway look in them now. "I don't know why I ran on like that to you. We've only met—what, twice before?" Elisa nodded her agreement. "Hell, I don't know the first thing about you."

"I have that effect on some people," she teased.

"What are you studying in graduate school anyway? I don't think you've ever told me what your plans are."

Elisa was not going to be so impolite as to remind him of the fact that he had not paid her the slightest attention on those other two occasions. Charlotte had made very sure—in a way only she could—that Garth's eyes never left her.

"Elisa?" Her name was repeated in a loud voice. It seemed obvious he was not used to losing his female audience.

"Oh, I'm sorry." She laughed to hide her embarrassment. "You asked me a question, didn't you? I'm a graduate student in psychology."

"Why psychology?" Garth asked interestedly.

"I guess I want to learn what makes people tick," she said simply. "Eventually I would like to work with children or in the area of family counseling." She did not expound on her reasons, realizing that, while it was a subject dear to her own heart, she found it bored most people.

Garth ran a hand through the thick thatch of hair that nearly met the collar of his jacket. "Huh, you've surprised me, Elisa Harrington, and it's been a long time since anyone has done that." Then the man turned his head toward the back porch. "I don't know how to tell you this, but we've got company," he commented in a lighter mood.

"Ophelia!" Elisa uttered her pet's name with impatient affection. "Oh, it's all right, I guess. Come here, you little dickens." She gathered the soft ball of fur up into her arms. "We'll have to swear him to secrecy, of course." She nodded in Garth Brandau's direction. "Do you like cats?" Two pairs of eyes regarded him with distrust.

"Of course," he answered diplomatically.

"Some people don't, you know. And Ophelia isn't supposed to be beyond that doorway. The poor thing was used to having the run of the house when she lived at the cottage. After all these years she still doesn't understand why the same privileges don't apply here." Elisa cradled the cat against her breast.

"Ophelia?"

"My father was a Shakespearean scholar and I, his most dedicated pupil. We considered them all—Portia, Desdemona, Rosalind. As a matter of fact," she told him with a straight face, "I'm lucky my name isn't Hermia or Calpurnia or—"

"—Puck?"

Elisa had to laugh. "Actually my father's first choice was Hermia, as I understand it, but he had to settle for naming the cat after the pathetic heroine of *Hamlet*. Mother insisted!"

"Thank God for your mother!" Garth heaved an exaggerated sigh of relief.

Ophelia seemed to meow her agreement.

"Would you like some more milk, my sweet?" murmured the young woman as she affectionately nuzzled her pet.

"Ophelia, you lucky dog!" Garth exclaimed wickedly, patting the small head, in the process unknowingly brushing his hand against the curve of Elisa's breast.

23

"D-don't say D-O-G in front of her. She'll get terribly upset," the girl scolded primly, trying to control the color that insisted on racing to her cheeks.

The man shook with laughter. "Practicing your psychology on felines now, Miss Harrington?"

Elisa lowered her voice to a whisper. "Ophelia doesn't know she is a cat. She thinks she's people."

"Really?" he whispered in turn. "Sorry. Hope I haven't given it away."

"Well, Ophelia." She straightened up with the satiated cat draped over her arm. "Time for your beauty sleep. Off to bed with you."

"Good night," Garth Brandau managed, with only a ghost of a smile breaking the serious line of his mouth.

" 'To sleep, to sleep: perchance to dream . . .' " Elisa recited with dramatic flair, sweeping across the kitchen, the languid gray form peering over her shoulder at the watchful man.

"Your father must have been an exceptional gentleman," Garth ventured upon her return.

Rather unwillingly she replied, "Yes, he was that. He died nearly ten years ago and I still miss him." Elisa had no idea why she admitted that to this man. She rarely spoke of Carl Harrington to anyone.

"I'm a little surprised you aren't following in his steps and studying Shakespeare."

Her dark eyes were sober as she floundered for the right words. "Don't you see, Garth? I had the best teacher there at home. My father lived and breathed his work: Shakespeare was something special between the two of us. I don't think I would want to share that with anyone else." She broke off, wetting her lips with a flick of her tongue. "I'm afraid I'm not saying this very well."

"You're doing fine, and I think I do understand. My father was a lawyer, and if there was one thing I *didn't* want to be, it was a lawyer."

From the tone of his voice Elisa felt he would not welcome any questions on the subject. "Would you like some more milk?" she asked, carton in hand.

"You're still a kid at heart, aren't you?" Garth tousled her hair as if she were. "Still a little wet behind the ears, Miss Harrington?"

It was the first time he had taken that condescending tone with her, and Elisa discovered she did not care for it one bit. Good God, surely he wasn't one of those men who consider all females of the species half-wits? She hadn't thought that of him.

"I can assure you, Mr. Brandau"—the young woman jerked the tie of her robe even tighter around her diminutive waist, not stopping to consider that her action would draw his attention to the way it outlined her figure—"I haven't been wet behind the ears, as you so charmingly put it, for a good while now!" Elisa looked up at him, her tone winter-cool, hands posed defiantly on her hips.

Hesitating, the man cleared his throat. "It would seem I was mistaken. You are most definitely a woman, Elisa Harrington."

Despite his sober appearance, she had the distinct impression he was laughing at her. "I would think that was obvious," she sniffed indignantly.

"Perhaps there is more behind those big dark eyes than just another timid female."

"I should hope so! What did you expect?" Elisa demanded.

"Sheath your claws, honey. Even you must admit that whenever I've been in this house you have been withdrawn and reticent in my presence," Garth reminded her gently.

"I suppose I have been," Elisa sighed, a graceful hand sweeping a stray lock of hair back from her face. "I've never felt totally comfortable with Charlotte's friends. I don't play tennis or backgammon or any of the things they

25

seem to do. We don't have anything to say to one another."

"You and I don't seem to be having that problem."

"Not now perhaps," she spoke into her hands.

"But if Charlotte were here . . ." Garth suggested with
a sudden flash of perception.

"I told you, Charlotte Rollins and I do not have a great
deal in common."

"How very formal you sound." The man cocked his
head to one side. "You're really not overly fond of her, are
you?"

"The feeling is mutual, I assure you. She considers me
an intellectual snob and socially naive," Elisa blurted out.

"And are you?"

"Am I what? An intellectual snob or socially naive?"
She looked wounded. "I'm neither, actually, although I
can't understand anyone going through life without just
once wondering what it all means. I suppose that sounds
horribly sophomoric to you."

"I may be ten years your senior, but I'm not completely
jaded. At least not yet anyway," he remonstrated, a wry
grin emphasizing his full mouth.

"Oh, but I didn't mean—"

"You have obviously led a sheltered, academic life,"
Garth pronounced.

"Only if you consider facing life and death a sheltered
life." Her voice vibrated with emotion she was loath to
reveal.

Garth Brandau studied her before speaking. "This time
it would seem I am the one who must say I didn't mean
it like that. I didn't, you know." He was forcing her to be
honest.

"I know," she finally said.

"Have you ever been in love, Elisa?" the man asked, as
casually as if he were inquiring about the weather.

She couldn't say why she answered him, but Elisa found

herself doing just that. "I imagined I was in love a few times."

"Imagined?"

"If you are referring to the kind of all-consuming love that reaches in and grabs your soul, turning you inside out so that nothing else matters—no, I haven't been in love that way."

"What dramatic creatures you women are," Garth mumbled, shaking his head. "Is that really the way you have found love? Or is that simply what you've deduced from your books?"

Elisa found herself blushing and on the defensive again. "You must have been in love a few"—she almost said "dozen" but reconsidered—"times. How do you see it?" There! Let him figure out an answer to that one! She pursed her lips with satisfaction.

"I'm afraid I see love as a great deal less earth shattering than you do, my dear. A man and a woman find themselves physically attracted to each other . . ." A nonchalant gesture of his hand finished the thought for him.

"In other words, Mr. Brandau, in your book it all boils down to sex!" Elisa was amazed by her own temerity.

"Did *I* say that?" His green eyes were wide and innocent as a babe's.

"Not in so many words, but then you didn't have to, did you?" She smiled at him sweetly. "Perhaps that is why you're thirty-whatever-you-are and still not married."

He came back quickly, without missing a beat. "In some societies, Miss Harrington, you would be considered an old maid."

Elisa took a deep, steadying breath. "I—I shouldn't have said that. I apologize."

"And I, as well. Let's declare a truce, shall we?" Garth said genially.

"*Pax!*" she conceded.

"*Pax* it is, then," the man repeated, offering his hand.

27

As Elisa went to put hers into Garth Brandau's she felt a yawn exerting itself. "Now, I've kept you up past your bedtime," he lamented, with a disapproving click of his tongue.

"No, really—" She started to protest, then caught the gleam in his eye. "You are an exasperating man, Garth Brandau!"

"You don't do badly in that category yourself." He chuckled appreciatively. "Don't think I haven't enjoyed our little chat, but I better let you get to bed."

"You look like you could use some sleep yourself."

"That wouldn't be an offer, would it, Elisa?" It seemed he could not resist one last shot at her.

"If it were, Mr. Brandau, you would have to be the last man on earth," she retorted with equal finesse.

Garth was still chuckling under his breath as Elisa escorted him to the front door.

"You might mention to Charlotte that I stopped by."

"I might," she replied, her hand on the doorknob.

"Definitely an exasperating woman!" she heard him mutter as he disappeared into the night.

For whatever reason, Elisa Harrington found herself smiling as she closed the door behind him.

CHAPTER TWO

Elisa opened her eyes and looked down at the book crumpled beneath her arms. She had evidently been resting her head on it. The young woman reprimanded herself: she was supposed to be studying, not sleeping! Final exams started in two days and it was imperative that she maintain the A's she had going in both of her classes this semester. She had come back for the weekend to work not sunbathe. But it was so lovely and lazy out here by the pool.

She sat up abruptly, pulling the beach jacket about her pink shoulders and pushing the pair of dark glasses back firmly on her nose. A brisk cool shower in her room and then she would get back to cracking the books—after a bite to eat.

Elisa reached out for her wristwatch on the table beside the lounger. Good Lord, four o'clock already and she had forgotten the lunch Millie had left for her. She scrambled to her feet, arms loaded with books, suntan lotion, and towel, and headed for the house. Haphazardly dropping it all on the back porch, she proceeded along the back

29

hallway to the kitchen. Dinner would not be served until eight o'clock and she was famished!

A frown creased her naturally arched brows. Come to think of it, she was always hungry these days. Thankfully the calories were burned up, keeping her figure slender and firm with no special effort on her part. All that dashing about from one end of campus to the other had to help, of course.

"Hello, Millie," she called out to the stout maternal figure whisking back and forth between refrigerator and stove. "Umm, something smells delicious!" Elisa exclaimed, peering through the glass door into the oven.

"You hungry, Miss Elisa?" the woman chuckled. "Well, if you weren't, then I guess I would worry."

"Oh, Millie, why can't you call me just plain Elisa? Why must it always be 'Miss Elisa'?" the young woman asked, one arm affectionately draped around the housekeeper's shoulders, a smile tying her mouth up into a bow.

"You are most certainly not plain, Miss Elisa. You're a very pretty girl and on the inside too, where it counts," the woman stated, deliberately misunderstanding her.

"You know what I mean." Elisa popped a freshly baked pecan tart into her mouth.

"In this house I have always called Miss Charlotte 'Miss Charlotte' and I'll do no differently with you, young lady." She shook her head emphatically, her hands expertly whipping a bowl of eggs and milk into a white froth. "By the way, I put back your sandwiches from lunch. You'll find them on the second shelf of the refrigerator."

Elisa raised her eyebrows in well-simulated surprise. "How did you know I missed lunch today?"

"I'm not blind. It was right there where I left it for you." Mildred Lawrence shook a finger at her reproachfully. "You don't look after yourself properly, Miss Elisa.

I was afraid of that when you moved out of this house five years ago," she sniffed.

"But I'm here now and you are a dear." The young woman beamed her an appreciative smile as she helped herself to the sandwiches. "Is Charlotte home yet?" The question came out between bites.

"Came through here nearly an hour ago. She was in a rare mood too, I'll tell you." But the grimace on Millie's face said otherwise. "I declare I don't know what's got into that girl lately. Not that she was ever an easy one to please, mind you, but nothing seems to suit her these days." She shook her head decidedly.

"Maybe what's got into her is a man named Garth Brandau," speculated Elisa. "Love does funny things to people, you know."

"Love, my foot!" the woman muttered, voicing her skepticism. "Mark my words, Miss Elisa, there's going to be trouble yet!"

Elisa unconsciously lowered her voice. "Don't you think Charlotte is in love with him?" She found the subject one of immense interest, when only the day before it had held none for her.

"It's infatuation, pure and simple!" On that final note— and it was final—the housekeeper clamped her mouth shut in an all-too-familiar manner. Once her mind was made up, there was no budging Millie Lawrence. The conversation was ended.

"Oh, my God!" Elisa's hand flew to her mouth. "Sorry, Millie, but I almost forgot. Garth Brandau came by the house last night while Charlotte was out. I'd better go tell her since he did ask me to pass on the message. I suppose she's up in her room." Large dark eyes were raised toward the ceiling, as if Charlotte's whereabouts could somehow be divined in the process.

"That's where she seemed to be going when I last saw her."

31

"I may as well get it over with, then, though I do hate to be around Charlotte when she's in one of her 'moods.' "

"Got too many dadburn moods if you ask me." The woman scowled.

"Thanks for the sandwiches. I think I'll survive until dinner now." She flashed Millie a bright smile.

"You're too skinny," the housekeeper tacked on as Elisa put her dish in the sink and headed back to the porch for her things.

Almost as if she were determined to put off the confrontation with Charlotte as long as humanly possible, Elisa stopped by her old room first, dumping the stack of paraphernalia on the desk before going through to the bathroom. She considered taking a shower, but settled for washing her hands and running a cool cloth across her face and a brush through the tangle of shoulder-length brown hair. Then, unable to avoid the inevitable any longer, she squared her shoulders and went along the upper hallway to Charlotte's door.

Knocking softly, she rather hoped the other girl might be napping and would fail to hear her. Evidently she was not to be so lucky.

"Yes" came the cool sophisticated voice from within.

"It's Elisa," announced the brunette as she opened the door and stuck her head in first. "Do you have a minute?" The rest of her then followed into the silk and lavender world of Charlotte's bedroom.

"Be my guest," said the willowy blond from her dressing table, where she had obviously been fussing with her hair. "I'd forgotten you were here this weekend. Actually I'm glad you dropped in. What do you honestly think of my hair this way?" Charlotte turned to face her.

For a minute Elisa was literally speechless. It was the first time she could recall Charlotte Rollins consulting her about any of the feminine frivolities. The young blonde

32

had always had an impeccable sense of what was right for her in any manner of dress or hairstyle.

"It's lovely," Elisa answered sincerely. "Your hair always is."

"You really mean that, don't you?" Charlotte drew her delicately marked brows together, then her face relaxed into a smile. "You're a funny creature sometimes. I swear there's not a jealous bone in your body."

"But jealousy is such a self-defeating emotion," protested Elisa.

"There speaks the psychology major," said the other girl, laughing. "Did you want to see me about something?" she prompted, returning to her styling efforts.

Whatever her mood upon arriving home an hour earlier, it certainly appeared that Charlotte was happy enough now.

"Yes, I forgot to mention it to you this morning. I mean you were in a terrible rush to get to your tennis game and it slipped my mind. Garth Brandau stopped by last night while you were out. He said something about finishing a big project he'd been working on. He wanted to let you know."

"Oh . . ." Charlotte looked at her in cool appraisal, causing the color to rise sharply in Elisa's face. "I hope you had the wherewithal to invite Garth in. Or did you keep him standing on the doorstep?"

"No, I invited him in," Elisa said quickly, falling into the trap before she realized it was a trap. Really, at her age she should have seen that one coming!

"Did you now?" the blonde said with a flicker of her blue eyes.

"Well, as you said yourself, I could hardly leave the man standing on the front step." Elisa defended herself with what she thought was admirable nonchalance. Far more nonchalance than she felt, in fact. Charlotte had always had this ability to put her on the defensive.

33

Charlotte spoke without anger, but there was a kind of icy coolness in her manner. "Why didn't Millie answer the door?" She appeared to be totally absorbed in filing her nails.

"She had already retired to her apartment for the night. Since I was in the kitchen having a snack, it only seemed reasonable to answer it myself."

"What did you say to Garth when he found out I wasn't here?" Charlotte asked without glancing up.

"Actually I don't believe I said anything—beyond the fact that I didn't know when you would be back, of course." Elisa flopped down onto the nearest chair. If she was going to have to give a blow-by-blow account of the entire evening, at least she could do it sitting down.

"You—ah—you didn't mention who I was out with, did you?" This was put to Elisa with the greatest of care.

"How could I? I hadn't the foggiest notion who you were with last night." Her tone was dry and a little brusque. But something began to take shape in the back of Elisa's mind. She had it! Charlotte didn't want Garth Brandau to know what she had been up to the previous evening. She was almost certain of it. "Who did you have a date with anyway?"

"Reggie Ashton."

"Oh, Charlotte, no!"

"No lectures, Elisa, I'm a big girl now."

"B-but Reggie Ashton—"

"Garth is a very attractive man, wouldn't you agree?" The abrupt switch in Charlotte's tactics threw her for a moment. "Yes, I suppose so," Elisa said uncertainly.

"Don't tell me tall, dark, and handsome, not to mention rich and intelligent, doesn't appeal to you," the blonde said with a faint cynical smile.

"I didn't say that." Elisa shifted her weight in the chair. "I'm sure in your book Garth Brandau is every inch the perfect male."

34

Charlotte laughed raggedly. "How little you know of men. It really isn't an act with you, is it?" Then she was suddenly quite serious, the veneer of sophistication gone. "Some men are so . . . self-contained. They would never understand someone who isn't, someone with weaknesses." The younger woman shook herself, feeling she may have revealed more than she intended. "Whatever did you and Garth find to talk about?" Her voice was brittle, the laugh forced.

"Oh, I don't know, I suppose he may have mentioned something about architecture, I told him a little of school, and we discussed the names of Shakespeare's women."

"Rather a lengthy conversation to be conducted in the front hall," Charlotte regarded her with Nordic blue eyes. "Or weren't you in the front hall at the time?"

"Well, actually—"

"It would seem you were the perfect hostess in my absence . . . perhaps too perfect. Did you invite Garth to join you for milk and cookies?"

Elisa quelled the outrageous urge to laugh aloud that bubbled up inside of her. "Actually it was milk and chicken salad."

Charlotte shot her a sly sideways glance. "Did he make a pass at you?"

For a minute Elisa could scarcely breathe. "No!" she choked out. "Why would you even think to ask such a question? What a dreadful thing to say about the man you're supposed to be in love with!"

"Let's just say I know something of human frailties." Charlotte's face was curiously animated. "Besides, there's more to you than meets the eye. A man like Garth might be attracted to the fact that you're different. He never could resist a pretty female under forty."

Elisa supposed it was rather a backhanded compliment. "He hardly struck me as a philanderer." She felt her palms grow warm. How ironic that she should be defending the man to Charlotte. "You're being terribly silly, you know."

The blonde's facial expression altered with startling suddeness. "Yes, I am, aren't I? It is silly to worry about other women in Garth's life. I'm young and beautiful and I can give him everything a man could want or desire." It was stated with self-satisfaction as she held up one hand for closer inspection. Then Charlotte glanced up at the brunette with clear and markedly innocent eyes. "You surely didn't take what I said seriously?" Her laugh was low and throaty.

"As a matter of fact I did." Elisa did not join in the laughter. "I don't happen to regard infidelity as a joke."

"You take life too seriously, you know. We're all human. It is perfectly natural for a man, or a woman for that matter, to desire someone . . . to want someone physically without the complication of emotion. Call it love, if you will. Haven't you ever wanted to go to bed with a man you weren't in love with?" Upon seeing the incomprehension in the other girl's face, Charlotte quickly added, "No, of course, you wouldn't have. It couldn't be any clearer if it were embossed in capital letters across your chest. You're an old-fashioned girl, aren't you? True blue and all of that. Dear God, your life must be dull!" This was uttered with just the right amount of ennui.

"It's not at all dull!" Elisa spouted. "I—I enjoy my studies. I have interesting, stimulating friends of all ages. I love to read and listen to Bach on rainy afternoons, or drink beer in the student union to Waylon Jennings, or dance all night." She wanted to add "Or feel the cool caress of water across my body when I swim in the pool," but this she did not confess out loud. "I cannot imagine anything more boring than jumping from one love affair to another." Elisa stopped abruptly. What had driven her to say so much to Charlotte when she didn't even like her?

"How do you know when you are really in love?" The

question was asked by Charlotte in all sincerity.

"I'm not sure, but I believe it's feeling whole and complete for the first time in your life . . . finding the other half of yourself. Someone who is friend and companion, as well as lover. Someone who understands you better than you do yourself sometimes. To be able to say that here is the man you will love for a lifetime and for whatever comes after."

Elisa noted the quick frown Charlotte gave.

"You're not asking much, are you?"

"I don't think so."

"Well, it's apparently not that simple or the divorce rate in this country would not be so atrociously high. There must be a hell of a lot of people out there getting married without all those pretty ideals."

"You missed the point, Charlotte. I don't presume to speak for anyone but myself. That is only my idea of love at its best. I'm not saying it's right for everyone. People get married for all kinds of reasons. But when I do get married, it will be because I couldn't imagine life without him."

"A hopeless romantic!" Charlotte laughed that superior, wiser-than-thou kind of laugh, but not before Elisa glimpsed a haunted, vulnerable expression flit across her beautiful face.

"I plead guilty then, but I don't mind somehow. The world just might be a better place if there were a few more of us romantics running around." Elisa put her nose an inch higher in the air. "It's all blatant sex these days, or so it seems. No more moonlight and roses. I, for one, rather like my moonlight and roses." She turned her head away before the impish grin on her face was visible to the blonde. At times it was simply easier to let Charlotte go on believing she was really that naive. It was a game she occasionally played.

"You poor thing." Charlotte Rollins's blond hair

37

swayed gently against her shoulders as she shook her head from one side to the other. "I can see that one day we'll have to be around to help pick up the pieces. You know what they say?"

"No, what do they say, Charlotte?" Elisa pressed her lips together.

"The bigger they are, the harder they fall!"

"I'll bet you thought that up all by yourself, didn't you?"

"Huh?" The girl's forehead creased perplexedly.

"Don't think I haven't enjoyed our little 'chat,' but I really must be going. I have tons of studying to do with finals coming up." Elisa stood to leave.

"Oh, thanks for taking care of Garth for me last night." Charlotte sought the last word.

Elisa Harrington's features relaxed into a smile. "Anytime."

Then she was gone before the young blonde could decide if she had been serious or not.

"Personally," said the young man with an exaggerated wink to one of his buddies, "I think I'm going to like this arrangement." His arm slid possessively around Elisa's shoulder as he leaned his head back against the booth. "God knows I've waited long enough for you to get out of that boardinghouse. It was run like a damn nunnery."

The color rose in Elisa's face like a flag. "Chuck Stephenson!"

One of the group offered a seemingly harmless snicker.

"That's enough out of you, Jim," Chuck half growled under his breath.

"Were you able to get the van for tomorrow?" Elisa inquired, putting a hand on his.

"No problem, honey," he said easily, his mouth softening as he gazed down at the young woman tucked under his arm.

"I hope you've lined up plenty of muscle," she teased. "It took three very burly movers to get that desk *up* the stairs."

When it was apparent that the others were not listening, Chuck murmured close to her ear, "I only wish I were going to be your roommate instead of Brenda."

"Behave yourself," she whispered furiously.

"That's no fun, sweetheart."

"Don't go getting any ideas, Charles Stephenson," Elisa stated, suppressing a grin.

"Too late for that at my age."

"You're only a year older than I am. That hardly makes you the elder statesman."

"Age has to do with a lot more than what year you were born." He seemed highly amused.

Elisa made an expressive grimace. "Are you implying that I'm backward for my age?"

"Let's just say there's a thing or two I could teach you. . . ."

"Right, Coach!" she laughed only inches from his mouth, knowing full well what was on his mind.

"What are you two whispering about?" cut in one of their friends. "You'd better watch him, Elisa. Next thing you know he'll be asking to see your etchings."

"Hell, I'll bring my own etchings if I have to!" said Chuck, laughing and drawing Elisa closer to him, her face quite pink by now. She had never been good at this kind of repartee.

"What's this 'penthouse' of yours like anyway?" asked a usually serious-minded graduate fellow named Mark. He directed the question to neither Brenda nor Elisa, but rather to both of them.

"While I would hardly describe it as a penthouse, it is on the top floor," answered Brenda tongue-in-cheek.

"Yes, on the third floor," Elisa added.

"The third floor?" echoed Chuck with a groan. "I don't suppose it has an elevator."

"Honey, we're lucky to have stairs!" Brenda exclaimed with good humor. "That desk of Elisa's is going to take up half of the living room."

"Fortunately," added Elisa. "So far it's the only stick of furniture we have for that room."

"Oh, I forgot to tell you," Brenda Collins's eyes lit up. "Mrs. Chalmers said we could have two overstuffed chairs and a coffee table from that vacant apartment on the second floor, bless her heart."

"I suppose you'll be needing some help moving those upstairs tomorrow too," Chuck muttered without any marked enthusiasm. "What a man won't do for love." The exaggerated sigh he gave was comical coming from a man of his size. As an undergraduate he had been the backbone of the front line, standing at least four inches over six feet and weighing nearly two hundred forty pounds.

"We promise you won't have to do it for love alone. Elisa and I will gratefully have a stack of sandwiches a foot high waiting for you and the 'team.' "

"Think you could manage a couple of six-packs of cold beer too?" he bargained shrewdly.

"Done! Cold beer as well," Brenda agreed, concluding the friendly negotiations.

"I hate to break up the party, but I've got to head for my last class," broke in Elisa, gathering her notebook and purse under her arm.

"I'll walk along with you," the man beside her said solicitously.

"Hmm, I've got to run too," gulped Brenda as she downed the last of her coffee. "See you all later."

"We'll meet at the apartment around ten o'clock," Elisa reaffirmed as she and Chuck were about to head in one direction and Brenda in another.

40

"Right . . . ten o'clock." The redhead waved cheerfully as she disappeared around the corner of the next building.

They had gone barely another ten feet when Chuck Stephenson stopped and turned her toward him, his bear-like hands resting on her shoulders. "Why don't you cut Professor Mueller's class and we'll go out somewhere?" he urged, gazing down into Elisa's face.

"I can't do that, Chuck. We're going over our final exams today and I want to take notes on the questions I missed."

"Ah, c'mon, Elisa, let loose and live a little!"

"Spring semester will officially be over for me in one hour. Can't you wait that long?" Her smile was benign, perhaps even a little maternal, as she put her head back to look up at the man who towered over her by nearly a foot. "We could go out later. I'm not working."

"Can't. I've got a wrap-up meeting with the coaching staff tonight," he mumbled, one hand leaving her shoulder to be raked through thick blond waves.

"I'm sorry, Chuck."

"No, it's all right. I guess your dedication is one reason why you've got where you are. I wasn't much of a student myself."

"You have a fine mind, Charles Stephenson. You just haven't always used it." It was a familiar theme.

"You've known me a long time, Elisa. If I'd lost my athletic scholarship, I would never have graduated at all. I still want to go to graduate school . . . someday."

"I know, I know," she said softly, and Elisa did too. "I better hurry, Chuck, or I'll be late for class."

"Oh, all right, honey, only . . ." As if he were driven by a force even stronger than himself, he pulled Elisa into a secluded alcove. He held her in his arms for a moment before claiming her mouth in a kiss that spoke of cherishing and desire and tenderness. "God, Elisa, you must know how I feel about you. You've got to know!" The

41

words exploded against her lips. "Come home with me and meet my folks. I know they'll love you as much as I do."

Chuck's words sent delicious shivers down her spine. It was intoxicating to feel this big muscular male tremble in her arms, to realize the effect she had on him as a woman. But whether it was some special feeling she had for Chuck that made her tremble in return or simply that her mind and body were telling her she was a twenty-five-year-old woman with all the normal desires, she wasn't certain.

"I really must go now, Chuck." Elisa laughed rather breathlessly, pulling away.

"A-all right. I'll see you first thing in the morning." He released her with obvious reluctance.

Elisa pressed a finger to his lips. "First thing in the morning, I promise."

She knew something was wrong the minute she pulled into the driveway. It was barely four thirty and yet James's and Amanda's cars were both there, and not particularly well parked either. The telephone message had simply requested that she stop by the house after class. Elisa got out of her old compact and practically raced up the front steps. She was still fumbling for her key when the door was thrown open by Millie.

"You've heard?" the housekeeper said without preamble, her face pinched into a scowl.

"No . . . h-has someone been hurt?" The young woman was almost afraid to ask.

"No, no, nothing like that, Miss Elisa," Millie hastily reassured her. "Mr. Rollins and your stepmother are waiting for you in the library."

"Thank you, Millie," she called over her shoulder as she dropped her purse on the nearest chair and went along to the library.

As Elisa entered the room Amanda Rollins rose from

her place on the sofa and came toward her. "We're grateful you came so quickly, Elisa," murmured the still attractive middle-aged woman as she hugged her stepdaughter, leaning on her for a moment as if she needed to absorb some of her strength. "James and I have had rather a nasty shock, I'm afraid."

"What is it, Mandy?" she asked, reverting to the childhood nickname she had always had for her.

"I blame myself in part for Charlotte's willfulness," sighed the graying man as he turned away from the window and walked toward the two women, his shoulders slumped in defeat. "If only she could have been more like you, my dear Elisa. Both feet on the ground, a good level head on her shoulders. You are a fine young woman, Elisa . . . a fine young woman." He stopped and put a trembling hand on his wife's shoulder. The three of them stood together, neither moving nor speaking for several minutes.

It was Elisa who finally broke the silence. "Amanda, what's happened? Is it Charlotte?" She led her stepmother back to the sofa and sunk to her knees in front of her, then she looked up at the man. "James?"

"It seems that Charlotte has run off with Reggie Ashton." It obviously caused him great pain to say the words.

"Run off?" Elisa's voice rang hollow even to her own ears.

"She has gone back to Europe with him," Amanda said through numb lips. "They didn't bother to get married first."

"Oh, no! James, I'm so sorry." Elisa rose and went to him, more stunned that he seemed to have aged years since she had last seen him than by the news about Charlotte. "Are—are you sure?" she inquired gently.

"Yes, there was a letter. It was left pinned to her pillow. Mildred discovered it this afternoon and had the good sense to call me at the office. After Amanda and I confirmed through a friend of mine at the airlines that they had left on a noon flight for Orly, we contacted Garth Brandau. He had just received a similar note himself. We—your stepmother and I—had the impression things were cooling off between them, but we never expected something like this. At least Charlotte had the decency not to leave it to us to tell him, though God only knows why under the circumstances."

"But why would she run off? And why with Reggie Ashton of all people? It's common knowledge that he has loads of charm and a fancy title, but not a penny to his name," Elisa thought out loud.

"We thought Charlotte barely knew him." Amanda's voice was a rasp.

"Her letter didn't make it very clear really. Some silly nonsense about loving his English accent and the fact that he put her on a pedestal. Worshipped and adored her like a goddess were the exact words. More likely it's Charlotte's money Ashton worships and adores," James Rollins told her bitterly. "If I ever get my hands on that no-good —" It seemed he had already forgotten his daughter's part in all of this. Perhaps that had always been one of the problems, Elisa thought to herself.

"Now, James . . . the man didn't exactly abduct Charlotte, did he?" Amanda seemed to be recovering some of the "salt of the earth" common sense she was known for. "What we must concern ourselves with is Charlotte's happiness. None of us wants to see her get hurt."

"Charlotte is a fool," murmured Elisa to one side. "How did Garth Brandau take the news?" she heard herself ask a little too eagerly.

"Damn decently," said James.

"He was concerned for Charlotte's welfare, of course, but otherwise he was exceptionally calm about it all," Amanda chimed in. "Garth is hardly a child, of course," she said unnecessarily.

"He wasn't angry?"

"He didn't appear to be, but then I'm sure he realized how upset Amanda and I were. No doubt he was trying to make it easier for us."

"No doubt . . ." Elisa hesitated, absently chewing on her bottom lip as if she didn't quite believe it. "Still, doesn't it seem odd to you that Garth wasn't upset?" She looked up at James Rollins. "I—I mean I was under the impression there was something between them. You would think the man would go after her if he cared." Why had she said that? What was it she hoped to hear these two poor people say—that Garth didn't love Charlotte? Why was she making such a point of his seeming indifference?

Amanda was adamantly shaking her head. "Garth Brandau doesn't strike me as a man who would chase after any woman."

"Well, I am!" James stated vehemently. "We have to go after Charlotte before it's too late." He looked down at his wife expectantly.

"Darling, don't you think it's already too late?" she said gently, not wishing to hurt him any more than he had been.

"Perhaps, but I could never live with myself if I didn't at least try to talk some sense into that errant daughter of mine."

"You're right, of course," Amanda conceded. "Charlotte must not be allowed to think that even this mistake isn't rectifiable. We must show her that we care, that she still has a choice, that we haven't closed the door behind her."

"I hoped you would understand. Thank you, my dear." The man bent over the back of the sofa and placed a grateful kiss on Amanda's cheek. "You really are an exceptional woman."

"I'll second that!" Elisa added fervently. "When do you suppose you'll try to leave for Europe?"

"Our passports are in order, thank goodness. With your

45

help and Millie's we could be packed by tomorrow." Amanda gazed up at her husband with that special kind of understanding a woman sometimes has for the man in her life. James needed to be busy right now above all else. "Darling, why don't you call and see if you can get us flight reservations? Then perhaps you should contact your office and make the necessary arrangements for the next week or two anyway. Miss Johnson will need to know what you want done about your appointments."

"I'll see to it immediately." His nod was decisive. The defeated posture was gone from his square-shouldered stance as he purposely strode from the room.

"Poor James." Amanda stared after him. "I didn't have the heart to tell him I think it's all a wild goose chase. But what about you, my dear?" The woman reached out to take her daughter's face between her hands. "About to move into your first apartment—and I'm afraid we're going to miss your birthday too."

"I'm going to be twenty-five years old next week, Amanda, not fifteen. I can't be a little girl forever. I have my job and summer classes and I've got to start work on my thesis. Besides, you and James may be back in a week with Charlotte in tow, for all you know. And if you aren't, you're not to worry." Elisa patted her hand affectionately. "Charlotte and James need you now more than ever . . . more than I do. Your place is at your husband's side. Heavens, I'll be so busy, I'll hardly know you're gone," she stated truthfully.

"Thank you, Elisa," her stepmother said simply.

"After all, what can happen?" The young woman smiled up at her. "I'll scarcely get my nose out of a book between my classes and working at the library. It's going to be a rather uneventful summer when it's all said and done."

But how little Elisa knew of what lay ahead for her. How little any of them knew.

CHAPTER THREE

"Good night, Elisa. See you on Monday," a tall, striking companion called out as they parted in the library parking lot.

Elisa raised a hand in response as she eased herself into her compact car, flicking the radio on just as the announcer wound up the eleven o'clock news. She had to admit she was weary, and little wonder: Sally Mullins had called in sick at the last minute and Elisa had worked Sally's shift as well as her own. After ten hours of filing, lifting, and bending, not to mention a full morning of classes, she was more than ready to head back to the apartment.

The extra money would come in handy, of course, she reminded herself. And why not work, even if it was Friday night? She didn't have a date and Chuck had gone home for the weekend to see his family, disappointed that Elisa had not agreed to accompany him.

The young woman pursed her lips in a thoughtful pose. There was no way of getting around it. If she had gone with Chuck, he would have read something into it that simply was not there between them. She could do without that kind of complication in her life right now.

There had been a letter that morning from Amanda. She and James were in Paris but would be leaving for Nice the next day. After nearly a week they still had not caught up with Charlotte and the infamous Reggie Ashton, seemingly missing the couple at every step. The runaways had evidently left Paris only hours before James managed to find out what hotel they had been staying at. She and James were trying to be discreet about the matter so that neither they or Charlotte would be embarrassed. With an added word about where they could be reached in case of an emergency, Amanda had closed with their love.

Elisa shook her head as she weaved the small car back and forth through the Friday-night traffic. She had to agree with her stepmother's initial sentiment: it looked to her like they were on a wild goose chase. After all, Charlotte was twenty years old. What she chose to do with her life was her own business. Yet, Elisa also understood James's concern for what he could consider only a mistake on the part of his impulsive offspring.

A scowl creased the young woman's forehead. There was something to be said for acting on impulse. Not that she ever had. At least not about anything monumental. Elisa Lynn Harrington had too much common sense, was too down-to-earth—a good level head on her shoulders, according to James—to do anything foolish on the spur of the moment. Perhaps that had always been part of her problem. Sometimes she wondered if she wouldn't be better off just *doing* instead of always *thinking* so much first. She did have a thing about being in control.

"You are getting fanciful, Elisa," she said in a mildly self-deprecating tone. "Just go home, have a nice glass of white wine, and call it a day."

She pulled into a convenient spot directly in front of the gray Victorian house—if one could call the large rambling structure built to accommodate a minimum of six apartments, a house. She parked with particular care, as there was an off-white Bentley just behind her. Garth Brandau drove a Bentley, very similar to this one, in fact.

Once again Elisa found her thoughts straying to the man, as they seemed to so often the past few weeks. Not having seen him since the night they had shared a snack in the Rollins kitchen, she wondered how he was taking Charlotte's defection.

Checking to be sure her car doors were securely locked, Elisa purposely walked up to the house, books in one hand, keys in the other, her handbag hitched over her shoulder. She let herself in the front entrance, a weary sigh escaping as she began the long ascent to her apartment.

Chuck and his crew had found out the previous Saturday just what a long haul it was to the third floor. But they had managed with relatively good humor to tug and heave and shove Carl Harrington's desk up each flight of stairs to the girls' apartment. The desk had been followed by the overstuffed chairs and coffee table from the vacant apartment on the second floor. At the last minute Mrs. Chalmers had donated a love seat as well. She apparently saw herself as some kind of self-appointed housemother, taking a special interest in each and every one of her tenants. Not that she pried; that was not her style either.

With their furniture finally in place, Brenda and Elisa had provided a reward of sandwiches, watermelon, and the promised ice-cold beer. It had been fun, thought the young woman as she trudged up the last flight of steps. After seeing Amanda and James off at the airport earlier that same morning, it had helped her to feel less alone to be surrounded by a group of caring friends.

It had not taken long, no more than three or four days, for the two young women to settle into a routine of attending classes, studying, and working. Brenda had luckily obtained one of the coveted positions as a cocktail waitress at a prestigious hotel, and so she was often gone in the evenings.

Elisa did not mind somehow being alone at those times. It gave her a chance to study without the interruptions that often resulted with another person in residence. She was well aware that the sometimes painfully outspoken redhead was in need of money even more than she was. The generous tips Brenda could look forward to would help provide the necessary funds for her graduate degree. Separate schedules and a general lack of togetherness were not problems for these two—both young women were used to being on their own. They wouldn't have wanted it any other way.

With a balancing act that would have been the envy of any juggler, Elisa maneuvered her key into the lock on the first try. She nudged open the door to the apartment, kicked it shut behind her, and walked across the pitch-black room, before some sixth sense, some indiscernible sound, told her she was not alone.

"W-who's there?" she whispered into the dark, clutching the key chain in her fist, ready to do battle if necessary to defend home and hearth, and her virtue, if it came to that. "I said who's there?" She was more angry than frightened by now.

"How like a woman to ask a perfectly ridiculous question," muttered a sleepy voice. "Just what in the hell would you do if I said 'burglar' or 'rapist'?" The voice was succinct and familiar and amused in an angry sort of way.

"I do not find that amusing, nor do I wish to carry on a conversation in the dark, *Mister* Brandau." She was really quite tired, and her sense of humor seemed to have deserted her somewhere on the stairs. With a flick of the light switch the living room was suddenly brought into focus. Elisa twirled around to face him. "So . . . it's you!"

"Hello, Elisa," drawled the man, his lazy smile conveying none of the irritation or surprise she was feeling. "Your roommate, Brenda—ah—"

"Brenda Collins."

"Yes, well, Miss Collins was kind enough to let me *in* as she was on her way *out*." A yawn interrupted the explanation Elisa felt she so richly deserved. Drat the man! Garth Brandau certainly looked at home sprawled in one of their armchairs. He had obviously been asleep or at least dozing. "Anyway, I told Miss—ah—"

"Collins," she repeated pettishly.

"Right! I told her I didn't mind waiting. What time is it anyway?" Garth ended on another yawn.

"You've got some nerve! After practically scaring the wits out of me, not to mention at least one year's growth, you can sit there and calmly ask me what time it is?" Elisa's voice rose several tones on the chromatic scale. "I don't believe this. I really don't believe this!"

She would have thrown up her hands in exasperation if they had been unencumbered. The young woman dumped her books on the desk, then stuffed her keys into her open handbag, before it followed suit. She stood facing him, arms folded in front of her, judge and jury rolled into one.

Although his eyes appeared closed, Elisa could feel the man watching her. It made her uneasy. She fixed him with large reproachful brown eyes, willing Garth to open his, to speak to her, to do something . . . anything . . . but he remained unmoving, immovable.

The dark green eyes flickered open in slow motion. His smile had that singularly intoxicating quality she remembered all too well. In a glance Garth Brandau took in the defiant figure posed in front of him.

"I believe you owe me an explanation, Mr. Brandau." She could be immovable too.

"Ah, come on, Elisa, surely you can bring yourself to call me Garth? If I remember correctly—and I do—you managed to use my first name the last time we met."

"You didn't scare the pants off me the last time," she reminded him, then silently chided herself for her unwise choice of clichés.

51

Garth hesitated and then said in a different voice, "Are you telling me I honestly frightened you?"

"Yes, you did." *Boy, he really catches on fast,* she said to herself with a smirk. "I am hardly accustomed to finding someone waiting for me in the dark," Elisa added with some indignation, biting down hard on her lower lip.

Great . . . just great! Another clever line to be misconstrued by someone with a mind to. The man was doubtless used to sophisticated, erudite women, not some little ninny who talked as if she had never had an original thought in her head. What was the matter with her anyway? But Elisa knew what it was. Instead of taking Garth Brandau as *she* found him, she was allowing the rumors and innuendos she had heard to color her thinking. It was something she prided herself on *not* doing.

Elisa could hear her father now: "Judge a man as you find him, not as others say they do . . . think for yourself, my dear, do not forfeit that right to anyone, for why else would God have given us humans a brain?" She could even picture in her mind's eye the kindly, slightly vague expression that always accompanied one of Carl Harrington's lectures. She hadn't minded his lectures, not even as a small child. She had soaked up every word like a sponge. Elisa had thought her father the wisest of men, recognizing that he wasn't like other fathers. Despite his apparent shortcomings as a parent, she had adored Carl Harrington right up until the day he died.

Garth caught hold of her unceremoniously by the shoulder. "Elisa, are you all right?"

"Hmm . . . did I drift off again?" she asked with eyes that did not see him.

He looked faintly puzzled. "Yes, you did. I'll admit keeping a woman's attention isn't a problem I've encountered before—until I met you, that is. Where do you go, for God's sakes?"

"I was remembering something my father once said

52

about thinking for one's self," she answered with a preoccupied air.

A shade of vexation passed over the man's features. "While I would no doubt have agreed with your father's sentiments, would you mind postponing your daydreams until another time?"

The girl looked up into his face, all trace of preoccupation gone. "What are you doing here?" She had nearly forgotten her earlier displeasure with him.

"Surely you don't expect a man to plunge right into long explanations without at least a cup of coffee to fortify him. You were far more hospitable at our last meeting," he hedged.

The man was damn disconcerting, Elisa admitted to herself. "You would like some coffee, then?" she inquired less than graciously.

"Yes, I would, please," answered Garth, stifling another yawn. "I haven't been to bed in forty-eight hours."

She noted the smudges beneath his eyes that had not been visible from across the room. "You look it too. You really should take better care of yourself, you know."

"Please—just coffee, no lectures," he said wearily.

"Yes, sir!" She very nearly saluted, then thought better of it and dropped her hands to her sides. His sense of humor might not extend that far on so little sleep. "You will excuse me." Elisa made a gesture in the direction of the kitchen. "I'll see to the coffee." Without waiting for any response from Garth Brandau, she turned and left the room.

From long experience the young woman efficiently went about the business of measuring water and coffee in the correct proportions. With the coffeepot starting to heat on a back burner, Elisa took two mugs from the cupboard, deciding she may as well join him. If the man wanted to talk, she was going to have to stay awake.

"By the way . . ."

53

At the unexpected sound of Garth's voice directly behind her Elisa nearly dropped the carton of milk she was taking from the refrigerator. She straightened up, setting the milk on the counter before she could bring herself to speak.

"For heaven's sake, do you always go around sneaking up on people?" she snapped at him.

"Sorry." He smiled ruefully, looking rather boyish all of a sudden. "You wouldn't happen to have a couple of sandwiches to go with that coffee, would you? I haven't eaten since breakfast."

"I'm sure I can come up with something if I try hard enough," she muttered tactlessly. "They don't take very good care of you."

"And who might 'they' be?"

"Oh, I don't know . . . your housekeeper or cook or whoever looks after your every need, your slightest whim," Elisa said waspishly.

"I have a woman who comes in several times a week to look after the place, but generally I eat in restaurants. As it happened, I was tied up in meetings all day right up until I came here around ten o'clock," explained Garth. "Look, if it's too much trouble, forget it." He threw her a withering glance.

"No, it's all right," she quickly relented. "I guess I'm just tired. It's been a long day. As a matter of fact, I could use a sandwich myself. I missed dinner too."

"Do you need any help?" he asked. It was a genuine offer.

"Thanks anyway, but this kitchen isn't big enough for the both of us." Elisa tried out a smile on him and was greatly relieved to see him return it.

"In that case, would you mind if I took a quick shower? I feel like I came into the world in these clothes." Garth glanced down at the expertly tailored three-piece suit he was wearing in a desultory manner.

54

Elisa's eyes followed his. Under the circumstances, she thought she had never seen a man look better. "Oh . . . n-no, go right ahead." She tried to sound casual, as if having a man shower in her apartment were an everyday occurrence. "I'm afraid I don't have anything you could change into—unless you wear a junior size seven," she heard herself tease him.

"I'll manage."

"The bathroom is down the hall on your right. You'll find fresh towels in the cupboard next to the sink."

"Thanks, five minutes is all I'll need," Garth promised as he disappeared.

It was nearly twenty minutes later by the time Elisa had the sandwiches prepared and the coffee simmering on low. It wasn't fancy fare—just egg salad and tuna fish, but it was the best she could do on such short notice. She absently nibbled on a dill pickle while she waited, impatiently vowing to give the man another five minutes, but not a second longer.

But when this five minutes had come and gone as well, Elisa began to wonder if something had happened to her guest. As was often the case in an older building, the plumbing creaked and groaned when in use. She had heard the shower go on and then off a few minutes later. Yet, Garth had not reappeared.

Elisa wandered down the hall toward the bathroom, stuffing the last bite of pickle into her mouth. Through the open doorway she could see it had been left as neat as a pin. But it was empty. The only indication that someone had even been there was a damp towel carefully folded and hung up to dry.

The young woman stood there in the doorway utterly bewildered. She marched back to the living room, but it, too, was empty. Where in the world was the man? Surely Garth wouldn't have left without saying something to her. No, she was certain she would have heard the apartment door being opened and closed, for it had a distinctive creak all its own. Then a second, less attractive, thought occurred to Elisa. What kind of fool did the man take her for anyway? What was his game?

She was a little hot under the collar now. Enough was enough. She was tired and hungry and definitely not in the mood to play silly games, not even with a man like Garth Brandau. *Especially* not with a man like Garth, Elisa though grimly. He was too old to be playing hide-and-seek.

Elisa made her way back down the hallway, past the deserted bathroom to the bedrooms. A quick glance determined that Brenda's was doubtless as she had left it on the way to work. A pair of jeans and a shirt were thrown across the end of the twin bed, but otherwise nothing was out of place.

Elisa nervously ran her tongue over suddenly parched lips, once, then twice. She took a deep steadying breath as she approached her bedroom, a queasy feeling causing her stomach to flop over in a most peculiar way, her heart pounding in her breast as though she had just run a marathon.

If this were a movie script, she could almost imagine the suspenseful music that would underscore a scene such as this. The innocent victim unsuspectingly going to her final demise. Someone or something always popped out from behind the door, usually with axe in hand. It had become a horror-film cliché.

The young woman swallowed a nervous laugh as she peeked through the crack in the door to see if a similar fate was in store for her. That was when Elisa Harrington got the surprise of her life—and the answer to all of her questions. For there—like in a perverted fairy tale—sprawled on his back across her bed, was Garth Brandau! And he was sound asleep.

A feather could have knocked her over. Garth had said

he was tired, but this was ridiculous. Well, he couldn't stay here. It was her room and her bed and she intended to use it herself. He would just have to find somewhere else to sleep, that's all there was to it! Yet Elisa found herself advancing into the room on tiptoe, oddly reluctant to wake him.

As was true of so many men, Garth Brandau looked younger, less threatening when asleep. Elisa stood by the bed watching the gentle rise and fall of his bare chest, the tangle of dark hair that formed a pattern across it, the perfect formation of his muscular torso. She understood perhaps for the first time why a woman would delight in being held in arms such as these. Power was emitted from the man even as he slept.

An idea popped into Elisa's head without warning, leaving her rather breathless. She had never been kissed by a man with a mustache. She wondered if it tickled. Thank goodness, Garth's was not one of those pencil-thin mustaches she always associated with Gilbert Roland and the 1940's movies, but neither was it a bushy, untamed thing. He obviously kept it trimmed, though she could not picture him primping and preening in front of the bathroom mirror. If anything, Garth's mustache seemed a natural part of his face, which she supposed was the supreme compliment to a man who sported one.

Elisa walked to the other side of the room without any special effort to be quiet and turned off the lamp on her dresser. The man did not move a muscle. She put the light back on and stood staring down at the inert form. At least Garth had had the foresight to put his trousers on after his shower. Be grateful for small favors! He must have been exhausted to have fallen so soundly asleep in what could only be a matter of a few minutes. But where did it leave her?

Common sense dictated that she simply wake him up, but as Elisa reached out to touch his arm something stopped her. A funny fuzzy feeling in the pit of her stomach, not unlike the time she had eaten too many green apples from Mr. McGuire's tree. Only it was not something she had eaten this time. It was desire, pure and simple, that made her draw away from Garth. Not his desire, but her own.

She jerked her hand back, her mind made up. She would leave him as he was, fairly certain he would not wake up until morning. Taking a spare pillow and blanket from the closet shelf, and her nightgown and robe from a hook on the back of the door, Elisa turned off the light again and shut the door behind her. She would attempt to make herself comfortable in the living room. Brenda would be home from work in a couple of hours and an explanation did seem advisable. But, oh, Lord, how *was* she going to explain Garth Brandau?

It did not take long for Elisa to discover that her five-foot-five-inch frame was not particularly well suited to a four-foot-long love seat. For seemingly the tenth time in an hour she turned over, vigorously punching her fist into the pillow. She felt a little better by telling herself it was Garth, uttering a rather unladylike opinion of the man who had commandeered her bed. No doubt he was comfortable enough!

The young woman sat up with a disgusted grunt. The luminous dial of her watch read nearly two o'clock. Brenda should be home any minute. At least then she could attempt to explain to her roommate about the man in the next room, though explanations would not miraculously make the lumpy sofa any more tolerable.

Elisa almost wished Garth had found his way to Brenda's room. At least that way the two girls could have shared her double bed. Ah, well, it was going to be difficult enough without having to inform her friend that "someone was sleeping in her bed."

She had just dozed off again when voices in the hall outside the apartment roused her. Elisa could discern Brenda Collins's country drawl and then the Eastern accent of her current boyfriend, Tony. He had been seeing Brenda home from the cocktail lounge every night this week—a sign of true love, in Elisa's eyes anyway. But this once she fervently hoped that Tony would say good night without coming in. What she had to tell Brenda was going to be awkward enough without a third party present.

Her hopes were shattered upon hearing her roommate extend an invitation for coffee, which Tony readily accepted. With gazellelike speed Elisa gathered up pillow, blanket, and robe and dashed for the relative safety of the hallway between bath and bedrooms. The telltale groan of the apartment door as it opened and closed drove her farther down the hall. There seemed to be no other choice. Elisa opened the door to her bedroom with exaggerated care and slipped inside.

She leaned back against the door, trying to collect herself, her breath coming hard and fast. Elisa closed her eyes. The doorknob digging into the small of her back scarcely registered. Then her eyes flew open. For a moment—but just for a moment—she had forgotten Garth Brandau's presence. A faint light issuing in through the windows enabled her to see the man on her bed. He had rolled over onto his side, one arm flung across both pillows. Otherwise Garth was as she had left him.

Elisa stood there shivering, the night air cool against her bare arms. It was a fine fix she'd got herself into this time. Here it was the middle of the night, she was dead tired, and worse, she had no place to sleep. And she was damned if she'd camp out on the hardwood floor! She would have to wait it out, hoping that Tony's cup of coffee in this case was instant.

If anyone had told Elisa that she could fall asleep on her feet, she wouldn't have believed them. All the same, her head kept nodding. She was tired right down to her bones. Cramps grabbed at her legs and back until she knew she must sit down.

The young woman gazed longingly at the empty space at the foot of the bed. Perhaps, if she were very quiet and very careful, she could sit there for a few minutes. Garth need never know. Placing the pillow to one side and with the comforter wrapped around her, Elisa eased herself down onto the edge of the bed. She scarcely dared to breathe. This was much better, and the man slept on, oblivious of her presence. Surely there was no harm in it. She gradually allowed herself to relax. God, she was tired!

Elisa Harrington never knew later what or who it was that brought her out of sleep, but when her eyes fluttered open to behold the sunlight streaming into the bedroom, she knew she had slept long and hard. She lazily turned over, stretching her arms in an arc above her head.

Dear God! She froze as she lay there, the air impelled back into her lungs with suffocating force. For there, next to her on the bed, was Garth Brandau. She realized then that the heavy band around her waist was his arm, and the breeze fanning her cheek was his breath.

Eyes as green as the sea in summer blinked open. He did not speak or move, but simply lay there staring at her, an indefinable expression flitting across his handsome features. What had she once said to herself about those eyes? "Bedroom eyes" she had called them. That was it! Under the circumstances, it seemed only too appropriate.

Her own studied gaze fell to the dark shadow on the man's chin. Not a weak, rounded chin, but one decisively sculpted there on his face with all the strength and solidarity of his character. Elisa had never been this close to a man first thing in the morning, unshaved, hair atousle, warm from sleep as he was. Of its own violition a slender finger reached out to touch his jaw, tracing a line from the well-shaped ear to the slight indentation on his chin.

Garth was not the one to shiver at her touch. It was Elisa who quivered as she came into contact with the man beside her.

Garth finally chose to break their vow of silence. "Hmm . . . good morning, Elisa. This is a pleasant surprise," he murmured, his breath stirring the stray wisps of hair about her face. He made no attempt to move away from her. "I see you decided to join me sometime in the night. I'm glad you did."

The young woman regarded him dubiously but could detect no mockery.

"Yes . . . I—I mean, no!" Garth's other arm came up around her, causing even greater confusion. "I-it's just that I was exhausted and the sofa was awful . . . and then Brenda had a friend with her when she came home from work. I couldn't very well explain about you being here, now, could I? So I slipped into my room. But they took so long and I couldn't stay awake. I m-meant to get up hours ago—" Elisa stammered to a halt, suddenly conscious of how breathless she sounded.

Garth drew a lazy pattern against her mouth with his thumb. "Has anyone every told you that you talk too much?"

"N-no, as a matter of fact, most people find me rather quiet," she confessed. Elisa was finding his touch far too disturbing for her peace of mind. "I—I don't know why I seem to go into lengthy explanations whenever you're around. I usually don't—"

Garth brought her up short with the most expedient method man has devised since it all began. He swooped down in ambush, covering her mouth with his in a kiss that shook Elisa right down to her unpainted toenails. It went through her like fire. She simply had no will to resist him, and in truth, it never entered her mind. When Garth moved his partially clad body to cover hers, she responded by softly groaning his name. There was no comforter be-

61

tween them now, only the flimsy summer nightgown she was wearing.

For the first time in her life Elisa Harrington was not in control of herself. It was the oddest thing: one minute she was, the next she wasn't. In one brief instant this man swept aside her every inhibition. She returned his kisses eagerly, her hands exploring new territories. Elisa discovered she liked the feel of his smooth muscular back beneath her fingertips, the riotous mass of hair that carpeted his chest, the strength in his arms that seemed capable of breaking her in two.

Garth's mouth began to do wild things to hers. His tongue teased her lips apart, drawing her down, down into the vortex of a searing embrace that proved all others before him to be amateurs in comparison. His hands outlined each curve of her as if committing it to memory. The strap of her nightgown was impatiently brushed aside as he trailed a line of scorching caresses across her bared neck and shoulder. His fingers found the rounded swell of her breast, bringing it to life under his tutelage. Elisa's name came from the man's lips over and over again until it finally penetrated the sensual haze surrounding her that she was not the only one who had lost control.

"God, this is crazy!" Garth grated through his teeth, obviously shaken by his response to her. "It isn't supposed to happen like this." He ran a hand through his hair in a standard gesture of disbelief. "You're just a kid."

"I'm not a kid!" she insisted through numb lips, daring at last to meet his skeptical gaze. "I'm a woman, Garth."

"Are you woman enough to understand that I want you?" he demanded without a shred of gentleness.

Before Elisa could formulate an answer, the man drove his mouth down on hers with a ferocity that frightened her. It was meant to be punishment for somehow making him desire her in spite of himself. She felt as if she had been cut adrift in an uncertain sea.

Elisa found herself responding to even this aspect of Garth's lovemaking, wanting him in whatever way he came to her. Then the storm subsided. The demon was exorcised. Hands that had bruised began to stroke. Lips that had demanded now asked. Persuasion was proving far more dangerous than force had ever been.

It was little wonder, under the circumstances, that neither Garth nor Elisa heard the persistent knocking at the bedroom door.

"Elisa, are you all right?" called out a concerned feminine voice. "I heard your radio go on, so I—I-yi-yi!" Brenda Collins stood in the open doorway, one hand raised to her gaping mouth.

Her roommate's untimely intrusion seemed like a douse of ice water down Elisa's back. She pushed Garth away and sat up to stare dumbfounded at the other girl, conscious of how it must appear to her friend.

Garth was the first to recover sufficiently to speak. "Ah, Miss Collins. Good morning," he managed in a conversational tone.

"I—I . . . excuse me!" The young woman backed out of the room with even greater speed than she had entered, her face the same color as her own fiery red hair.

"Brenda, wait!" Elisa called after her too late. "Oh, no," she groaned into her hands, unable to face even herself just at that moment. "What can I possibly say to make her understand?"

"I think she understands perfectly well. After all, we weren't exactly playing gin rummy," Garth reminded her unnecessarily.

"B-but it looked like we were—were—" She was averse to putting it into words.

"In another five minutes we would have been," the man said, closing his mouth firmly. He evidently did not believe in pulling any punches either.

"I don't think I care to talk about it right now, if you

63

don't mind." Elisa turned away from him and slipped off the bed, trying to scrape together some of her former self-respect. She had never reacted to a man like this before. Her mind and emotions were in a turmoil and rightly so. "I—I want to speak to Brenda." Her voice held an unsteady note. Elisa grabbed her robe and dashed from the room before Garth could say or do anything to stop her.

She found her roommate in the kitchen, going through the motions of making herself a cup of coffee. Elisa gave a self-conscious laugh. "You're stirring that to death."

The petite redhead swung around to face her, remnants of a blush still visible on her cheeks. "Oh, Elisa, I'm so sorry! I would never have barged in like that if I had had any idea—"

Elisa interrupted her with a wave of her hand, wanting, needing her friend to believe what she had to say. "I'm the one who should apologize, Brenda. It wasn't what you thought. Honestly it wasn't." Her voice was low. Her hands nervously tied and retied the belt of her bathrobe. "I know what it must have looked like to you, but it—it wasn't."

"She is absolutely right, you know." Garth's deep masculine voice spoke from directly behind Elisa as his hands came down on her shoulders in a possessive gesture. He looked from one girl to the other. "I think we should let Brenda in on our secret, honey, don't you? I can see she's concerned for your happiness, like any good friend."

"Secret?" Elisa sounded faintly dismayed. Something in the man's voice set off warning bells in her head. She turned around in his arms. "Garth?"

Garth Brandau ignored the question in her puzzled brown eyes and continued. "You can be the first to congratulate us, Miss Collins. Elisa and I are engaged to be married."

CHAPTER FOUR

Brenda Collins looked from her roommate to the attractive and rather striking man standing beside her, then back once more to the pale young face of her friend. "Engaged? You're engaged?" Disbelief and shock battled for first place on her own pink-tinged countenance.

The man's fingers bore down into Elisa's shoulders in warning. She felt a little tingle of pleasure at his touch, and then at once berated herself for it.

"Yes, Elisa and I are engaged." An edge of steel underlined Garth's voice. "We hadn't planned to tell anyone just yet, but under the circumstances, I think you deserve to know that I am going to make an honest woman of her. I'm afraid Elisa and I may have given you quite a shock earlier." Then he laughed. A long, rich, deep laugh.

Elisa shook herself. She couldn't believe what she had heard. It was incredible! And the man actually seemed to be enjoying himself. Surely he hadn't just told Brenda they were engaged? Why, it was the singularly most ridiculous thing she had ever heard. Things were happening far too quickly.

"B-but Garth . . . it really isn't necessary," Elisa stammered.

"I think it is, *darling,*" he replied, his voice quiet, dangerously quiet.

"Well, then, congratulations and best wishes, of course," Brenda said after the briefest of pauses.

"Thank you, Miss Collins." Garth bestowed one of his most charming smiles on the young woman.

Elisa contrived to raise an answering smile. She never knew if she succeeded. But she had news for Garth Brandau. Theirs was going to be the shortest engagement on record. She realized only too well that she did not have the nerve to confront the man with his fantastic lie in Brenda's presence, but just as soon as she got him alone again—Well, that would be another story altogether.

Brenda ventured a glance at the kitchen clock and uttered an involuntary gasp. "Oh! You two will have to excuse me. I've got to run." She quickly rinsed out her coffee cup in the sink. "I'm supposed to meet Tony in fifteen minutes." As she went to leave, she finally looked her roommate square in the face. "Do you think you might be in for dinner tonight?"

"No, she won't," Garth answered for her.

"I'll leave you a note if I decide to go out," Elisa added boldly. There was no reason why Garth Brandau should have it all his way.

"Until later, then. It was nice seeing you again, Mr. Brandau," Brenda murmured self-consciously as she slipped past him.

"My pleasure, Miss Collins," he returned affably.

Elisa felt a bitter taste rise in her throat. It seemed that even her usually caustic friend was taken in by the man's charm. Was no woman immune? It was particularly galling since she knew that Brenda was often scornful of smooth, sophisticated men like Garth Brandau.

Then the young brunette woke up to the fact that she

was once again alone in the apartment with Garth. She impatiently shrugged her shoulders. For some reason she did not care to examine too closely, the thrill of his touch had been replaced by annoyance. She may have even stamped her foot, but since her feet were bare, the gesture proved more comical than indignant. Nevertheless the man's hands fell away.

Elisa spun around, anger darkening her brown eyes and coloring her cheeks, her hair in wild disarray.

"And just what in the hell was the big idea of telling Brenda we were engaged?"

Garth left her question unanswered and instead asked one of his own. "Why? Is the idea that repugnant to you?"

The girl made herself count to ten before she replied, "I hardly think that's the point. What I want to know is who gave *you* the right to make an announcement like that without my permission?"

"Look, would you mind if we postpone this discussion until I've had at least one cup of good strong black coffee? I never did get my sandwiches and coffee last night, you know."

"Oh, you and your darn coffee!" she grumbled. Elisa would have dearly loved to slap that complacent expression from his face. "You—you—"

Garth placed a finger against her lips, looking down at her as if she were an exasperating child whose antics he could do without. "I don't like to hear a woman swear, Elisa, especially a pretty young woman." His voice snapped with authority.

"I will do and say what I damn well please, Garth Brandau!" She carefully enunciated each word. "If you don't like it—Well, you know what you can do!"

The man gave a grunt that may have been a laugh. "My, my, here we are scratching and fighting like cats and dogs. Anyone would think we were married."

"Y-you're crazy! Do you know that? What does it take

to get it through that thick skull of yours? There *is* no engagement. There will *be* no engagement. Not now. Not ever!" Elisa was nearly shouting at him.

"I think the lady doth protest too much."

"Oooh, I would love to get my hands around that neck of yours," she muttered under her breath, her slender hands unconsciously making wringing motions.

"While I admit there have been a number of women rather anxious to get their hands on me," Garth chuckled in a suggestive way, "it wasn't in that context."

"No conceit in your family—you've got it all," Elisa taunted in a childlike, petulant voice.

The man actually seemed offended by her barb. "I don't think it's conceited to see things as they are, to believe in yourself, to possess a healthy dose of self-confidence."

"Perhaps. But there's a fine line between conceit and confidence. Or hadn't you heard?" she mouthed with apparent relish.

"You are a sharp-tongued little witch, aren't you?" Garth slowly ran his fingers across her lips. "I prefer your mouth beneath mine, kissing me as though there were no tomorrow . . . as if we had never been strangers."

Elisa flung up a defiant chin. "I would prefer you keep your hands—or whatever else—to yourself."

"I know why you're angry and on the defensive, honey," he said in a soothing tone. "I promise we'll talk just as soon as I've had that blankety-blank cup of coffee you mentioned ten minutes ago."

"You brought up the subject of coffee, not me."

"Dammit, Elisa, don't be so contrary!"

"Sorry, *sir,*" she snickered, dipping him a little curtsy. "I do so hate to hear a man swear though, Garth. Especially a handsome, if not quite young, man."

"All right, you've had your fun. Now run along and put some clothes on." It was a definite dismissal.

"Have I told you that you're beginning to get on my nerves?" Elisa said in a tone of concentrated fury.

"I will be on more than your nerves if you don't get dressed," he promised, out-of-patience. Then a crooked, sensuous smile spread along his face. "You know, my dear Elisa, you are tempting in that silky little number you're wearing." One finger flicked at the exposed strap of her nightgown.

The young woman slapped his hand away, turning up her nose. "Flattery will get you absolutely nowhere."

"Then I suggest you get going, honey."

Elisa struck out at him, showing no sign of compliance. "Don't you 'honey' me, Garth Brandau! And don't tell me what to do either."

With an exasperated sound he silenced her with a swift, hard kiss that left Elisa's senses reeling.

Garth tore his mouth away with some reluctance. "For my sake, if not your own, please get dressed. I'll put the coffee on and see what I can rustle up for breakfast."

"B-but Garth . . ." Elisa looked at him wide-eyed and wondering, one hand raised to the trembling lips he had just given another lesson in passion.

The man proceeded to repeat his action, but this time the kiss soon turned to gentle persuasion, seducing the pink mouth into surrender. Garth seemed to be asking more of her than just capitulation. He wanted her to be an equal partner in desire.

"Ah, to hell with it," Garth breathed raggedly against her mouth. "We can always have that coffee later."

Elisa pushed on his chest, finding untold strength in her arms. "N-no, you go ahead and put the coffeepot on. I—I'll get dressed now."

"Running away, Elisa?"

Her step faltered. "Yes!" she confessed in a moment of truth before continuing on her way. Once she was safely within the confines of her bedroom, she breathed more easily. There was a dangerous man!

She gave little thought to her appearance, quickly pulling on a pair of designer jeans—a birthday present from James—and a cotton T-shirt. After all, the prime objective was to get dressed and *fast*. It wasn't that she didn't trust Garth not to barge in on her . . . but she didn't.

Elisa dropped on all fours to rummage about the floor for her favorite pair of sandals—the ones with the two-inch heels. In the face of adversity she had always felt that taller was better. Then she flopped down on the edge of the bed to secure the thin spaghetti straps around her ankles. Out of the corner of her eye the girl glimpsed the rumpled pillows side by side. For a moment she could almost visualize her own dark head there beside his.

Elisa shot off the bed. Damn! What had she got herself into? Her life was neat and tidy, and she preferred it that way. She even knew precisely why.

Elisa Harrington had once described herself to a friend as a nice-enough-looking girl with a good mind. She had been taught that to waste a good mind was an unpardonable sin and she believed it. After graduating from the university at twenty-two, she had worked full-time for nearly eighteen months to get the money to start graduate school. It hadn't been enough, of course, but a part-time job combined with part-time class work had proved to be the answer. One more semester and then her thesis. She planned to sit for her orals in the spring. She had her future mapped out and only by single-minded determination would she succeed.

Now, in the space of a mere twelve hours, her world had been turned topsy-turvy, inside out, upside down. Elisa felt as if she had somehow inadvertently stumbled into someone else's dream. She needed time to collect herself, to sort it all out.

"You'd better think about it while you scrub your teeth,

or he may be in here after you," she muttered under her breath on the way to the bathroom. She was just a little bit frightened of Garth Brandau.

It was while she was vigorously brushing her hair that it came to Elisa. She had been trying to pinpoint the exact moment when Garth had become a viable force in her life. She decided it was from the time she walked into the apartment last night. Garth had been different and she had too. They had met last night as man and woman.

Elisa made a face at herself in the mirror. "You know it was a lot safer the other way."

"What was a lot safer?" Garth's reflection joined hers in the vanity mirror.

She stuck out her tongue at him in answer.

"In that case, do you intend staying in here all day or would you like to join me for *le gourmet* breakfast?"

"Don't tell me you can cook?" she asked with a light-hearted laugh. The vision of Garth slaving over a hot stove was amusing.

"I may not be Julia Child—"

"You are most certainly *not* Julia Child," she interrupted him with a hoot. "James Beard perhaps . . . Julia C. never!"

"At least I can put together enough to keep us from starving."

Elisa's hand flew to her mouth. "Oh, my gosh, you haven't eaten since yesterday morning."

"You remembered," he said wryly. "Then you will understand that while I would normally like nothing better than to stand here talking to you, I'd rather eat my breakfast right now." He took her firmly by the arm and half dragged her to the kitchen. "Sit there!" he ordered, plunking the girl down on one of the two kitchen chairs.

"Hmm, it looks good," Elisa said in appreciation as Garth set an egg cup and lightly buttered toast in front of

71

her and another by his own place. Two steaming mugs of coffee followed.

"It was the best I could do with what you had on hand. One day soon I'll stock my own refrigerator and make you my specialty."

"And what, pray tell, is your specialty?"

"Soft-boiled eggs and toast," he laughed.

Their laughter shattered the tension in the room into a thousand tiny pieces. Elisa found herself relaxing. She ate with surprising heartiness as well. It was while she sat back leisurely sipping a second cup of coffee, watching Garth consume his third egg and fourth slice of toast, that she tried once more to approach him on the subject of their "engagement."

"We've got to talk, Garth." She leaned forward in her chair, her tone insistent.

"Of course, and we will." But his manner was basically one of unconcern.

"I meant *now!*" Elisa said, deciding to take the offensive.

"Huh." The man honored her with a grunt.

Struggling to express herself, she went on. "Perhaps you made that—that ridiculous announcement this morning thinking it would somehow protect my reputation. I can assure you the situation did not call for such a drastic solution." Elisa could sit still no longer. She rose from the chair to pace back and forth in the small kitchen.

"There are still men of honor who believe they should make things right if they compromise a lady."

Elisa pulled up abruptly and swung around to face him. Surely he was making fun of her. That kind of chivalry had gone out of style with chain mail. "This was all unnecessary, you know."

"Are you trying to tell me this wasn't the first time Brenda has found you in bed with a man?"

The brunette lifted her chin, a look of pure fury in her

eyes. "Of course I'm not saying that! There are women who think more of themselves than to sleep with any old Tom, Dick, or Harry who comes along. What I'm trying to tell you is Brenda would have understood if you had given me a chance to explain. She knows I'm not the type to sleep around. Everything would have been fine if you hadn't butted in. Now you've made a real mess of it!" Elisa reproached him. "When Brenda gets in later, I'll tell her exactly what happened—or didn't happen. This so-called 'engagement' of ours will be one mistake only the three of us need ever know about."

Garth gave her a quick shrewd look. "You've got it all figured out, haven't you?"

"Yes, it's quite simple really. Oh—and don't worry, I'll be sure to mention the chivalrous sacrifice on behalf of my honor." Her voice vibrated with the last word.

"What about my car being parked out front all night?"

"P-perhaps no one noticed."

"Where did your roommate go today? Do you know?"

"Why?" she asked suspiciously.

Garth's face darkened with ready anger. "Can't you answer even a simple question without making it sound like I'm planning to ravish you? What happened this morning wasn't one-sided, you know."

"I—I know," admitted Elisa, wishing somehow it wasn't so. "Brenda usually goes to the university library to study."

"That wasn't so difficult, now was it?"

"No."

"My point is do you honestly think that by now our engagement is still privileged information?" Garth obviously thought her incredibly naive.

A rapid sinking feeling ran through Elisa. "Damn! I didn't think of that," she said with sort of a groan. "Brenda will tell everyone she sees." The groan became a wail.

"We didn't ask her to keep it to herself. It's only natural

she would want to spread the 'good news.' And I for one do not care to look the complete fool. With all due modesty, I am rather well-known at the university."

"What do you suggest for our next move, then?" she sighed dejectedly.

"As I see it, there's only one thing we can do: stay engaged a respectable length of time and then at some satisfactory date in the future mutually call it off." He made the idea sound almost logical.

"Won't a fiancée cramp your style?"

"No more than a fiancé will yours."

"Oh, I don't know . . . I guess you mean well enough."

Fool! Garth Brandau was one of the most attractive men she had ever met and she was behaving as if he were some repulsive hairy-ape type. Under any other circumstances she would have enjoyed dating a man like him. *Don't put it under a microscope to examine every detail,* she scolded herself. *Don't analyze it to death. For once just do it! Go on, Elisa, live a little. You're twenty-five years old. Be impulsive!*

"Well, what do you say, Miss Harrington?" He was waiting for her answer with the closest attention.

"All right," she said ungraciously.

"Good! Now for the ground rules," Garth went on. "I think it would be wise to act like a normal engaged couple. Hence, we will go out together, be seen together, and may all of our friends be platonic." He seemed to think he had put that rather cleverly.

"Oh, no, I forgot all about Chuck!" the young woman said aloud, but to no one in particular.

"I wouldn't much care for that if I were Chuck." Garth Brandau's eyes burned like coals. "Who is he?"

"Chuck Stephenson, a f-friend from my undergraduate days. We've dated off and on for years."

"Wasn't there an all-American here at Wisconsin by

that name five or six years ago? Got hurt pretty badly at the end of his senior year, if I remember correctly."

"Yes, that's Chuck. It ruined any chances he had for a pro career. He's an assistant coach now. Chuck has been trying to get me to go home to meet his folks for months. He's never going to understand no matter what I say." The thought was less distressing than it should have been.

The man's reply was quick and firm. "Perhaps not ... but you will tell him absolutely nothing of the circumstances of this engagement. If we go through with this, I expect you to behave like a loyal, loving fiancée. There will be no old boyfriends waiting in the wings for the curtain to come down."

"Does that go for you as well? No old flames ready and willing to light your fire?" Elisa burst out giggling but broke off at the sight of Garth's serious face.

"You're not really serious about this guy, are you?" He seemed determined to return to the subject of Chuck Stephenson.

"He's nice."

"Nice?" Garth repeated, in a low mocking tone. "You're not, then. No woman describes the love of her life as 'nice.'"

"I would certainly never describe you as nice, make no mistake!" Elisa blurted out with no thought to what it might convey to this man. Then her expression changed to one of puzzlement. "Why are you doing this, Garth?"

"Perhaps I fancy you," he replied in that deep sonorous voice of his.

"A likely story, Mr. Brandau," she said, chuckling. "But you never did tell me what you were doing here last night." She pursued the matter.

"Believe it or not, I simply found myself wanting to see you."

It was not the answer Elisa had expected to hear.

"Look, honey." Garth put a hand on each of her shoulders and gazed straight into the dark troubled eyes. "I am still in the same clothes I put on at six o'clock yesterday morning. I need a shave and a shower. I would like to brush my teeth. Now I want you to go collect your purse or whatever you'll need for the day while I clean up the dishes. We're going over to my place so I can change. Then I'm taking you to lunch, Miss Harrington." He spelled it out for her step by step.

"Lunch? But I'm not dressed to eat out!" she wailed in typical female fashion.

"You look fine. The restaurant I have in mind is very casual. Now scoot!" Garth flicked the dishtowel at the back of her retreating form.

Elisa tossed her loose brown hair back from her shoulders. "Your aim seems to be off, Mr. Brandau," she taunted, as if she were not the least bit afraid. "You missed me completely."

"Did I?" She saw a flash of white teeth. "In that case I'll have to try harder next time. You have my word on it, Elisa Harrington."

There was something in Garth's eyes she did not fully understand . . . did not want to understand. Elisa fled before he could change his mind, having no doubts the man was as good as his word.

Elisa had assumed that Garth had money. The Brandau name and wealth had always gone hand in hand. Then there were the obvious, if tasteful, accoutrements: the perfectly restored Bentley, the expensive hand-tailored clothes, the chic restaurants where he had seemed to take Charlotte, the exclusive country club. But nothing had prepared Elisa for just how rich he was as Garth pulled up in front of the fashionable address and escorted her via a private elevator to the top-floor apartment he called home.

"Good Lord!" she blurted out like some unsophisticated schoolgirl, then immediately wished she hadn't. She hated being impressed, but she was all the same.

"Do you like it?" the man casually inquired as he closed the door behind them.

"Well, it certainly has all the trappings." There was a slight edge to her voice. "A real Renoir?" She had turned to study the painting on the wall beside her.

"Yes, it is an original," he answered her, as though an original Renoir hung in everyone's home.

The young woman nearly laughed out loud. Why, it was ludicrous to even call her apartment and his by the same name when they were so obviously worlds apart. The tiny four-room flat she shared with Brenda could not compare with the sprawling luxury she saw here. It was without a doubt the swankiest setting she had ever seen this side of the movies. And somehow the veneer of wealth displayed all around her made Elisa think just a little less of the man. She had thought . . . hoped . . . that Garth might be different from the others.

"You really are one of the Brahmins of the world, aren't you?" Her voice was a thin strip of incredulity. "It will never work, you know," Elisa sighed without being conscious that she did so.

"What will never work?"

But she had a feeling Garth knew exactly what she meant.

"An engagement between you and me, however contrived. I'll admit I hadn't thought of it before, but a man in your position will undoubtedly make the newspapers with an announcement like that. I can see the headlines of the social page now: 'Madison's Most Eligible Bachelor Snared by Little Nobody.' You wouldn't like it any more than I would. All of your friends would know, and your family. It was an absurd idea. You must see that yourself."

"I don't see that at all. What the hell is this—reverse snobbery?" Garth was angry with her. "I don't give a damn what the social gossips say, and I have no family besides my mother and a few distant cousins. My friends will adore you, or they aren't much in the way of friends." He dispensed with her objections as quickly and easily as most men might flick an insect from their hand. "Now before that overactive imagination of yours comes up with anything else, I'm heading for the shower. Make yourself at home," Garth called from the doorway, one hand already undoing his tie. "There's juice and cola in the refrigerator. Open cupboards or whatever until you find what you want. *Mi casa es su casa.* I'll join you as soon as I'm human again." A moment later the man poked his head back around the corner of the room. "Feel free to look around . . . if you would like to, that is." Then he was gone again.

Elisa tentatively took a step further into the luxurious surroundings. The main room was decorated in shades of brown and red. As she was to discover later, the color scheme ran throughout the entire apartment, all six rooms —two bedrooms, dining room, living room, kitchen, and study, not to mention the largest walk-in closet she had ever seen and two marbled bathrooms. The Oriental influence was predominant, but contemporary touches here and there, like the Renoir, blended in well.

She found the kitchen on her second try, the first having dead-ended at what she could only assume was Garth's study. It was an intriguing book-lined room that possessed not only a large ornate desk, but a drafting board, where she could make out a half-finished drawing. She might have been tempted to take a closer look, but the study somehow had PRIVATE indelibly stamped on it. It would have to wait until another time . . . if there was another time.

The kitchen in which Elisa found herself, though compact, had every modern convenience. Deciding a cold drink would be welcome, she took a glass from the cupboard and added ice and cola from the refrigerator. It gave her something to do until Garth returned.

Drink in hand, she wandered through the dining area back to the living room, enjoying an almost sensual reaction to the surroundings now that she let herself. The carpet was thick as a meadow in midsummer. The drapes blended with the wall covering to create the effect of bringing the very sky into the room. There was a serenity here that caught Elisa unaware. She curled up in an overstuffed chair that almost seemed to swallow her up into its softness. The young woman put her head back and closed her eyes, letting the tension that had been building since the previous evening slowly dissipate.

"I see you've found what you wanted," Garth said softly from somewhere nearby so as not to startle her.

"Have any of us found what we really want?" she murmured pensively. Then Elisa sat up straight in the chair, or as straight as it would allow. "Oh, yes, thank you," she said, reaching for the drink she had scarcely touched. "Are you going to join me?" Elisa indicated the glass of cola.

"No, I'll wait until we get to Luigi's."

"Luigi's? You mean you were serious about lunch?" She gave a short laugh.

"Naturally."

"But how can you possibly be hungry already?"

"Easily. I just am. Breakfast merely whetted my appetite. Your kisses do the same thing to me. They leave me wanting more," said Garth, concentrating on her mouth.

"You don't really get results with lines like that, do you?" she asked, giggling.

"How do you know I'm not serious?"

"I—I guess I don't." Elisa's laughter died away. "But then, I don't know very much about you at all, do I?"

"Then I will gladly begin to enlighten you over lunch." He smiled at the girl.

Luigi's was one of those cozy places tucked away one flight below street level. No flashing neon lights announced its presence, only a discreet hand-lettered sign in the café-curtained window. It was small, intimate, and immaculate. A shiny jukebox sat in one corner, and as Garth pointed out, it played only traditional Neapolitan songs, from "Arrivederci, Roma" to "O Sole Mio." There were no printed menus, not at Luigi's. There was, however, an autographed eight-by-ten glossy of Mario Lanza proudly displayed by the kitchen door.

"Buon giorno, my friend. *Avanti! Avanti!"* Luigi called out, as he came forward to greet them himself. He took Garth by both arms and hugged him vigorously.

"Hello, Luigi. I've brought my fiancée to try your excellent lasagna. I hope you made a fresh batch this morning."

"But of course! Your fiancée, huh?" The man's eyebrows rose expressively.

Garth did the honors. "Miss Elisa Harrington . . . Luigi Lorenz."

"You are most fortunate, Miss Harrington. Felice, my daughter, and I have just finished the pasta. The first pan of lasagna will be out of the oven in thirty minutes, perhaps less." He turned his attention to Garth. "So, my young friend, you are finally going to take a wife. Remember what Luigi tells you: Never go to bed angry. It has served my Anna and me well for forty years. You remember Luigi's advice and you will live long and happy."

"I'll remember, my friend." Garth tossed his head back and laughed.

"Now I leave you two lovebirds alone. I will send the waitress, one of my nieces, with some wine and antipasto." Then the man disappeared as quickly as he had originally appeared.

"I hope you like lasagna," Garth whispered in her ear as he settled Elisa in her chair. "It would break Luigi's heart otherwise."

"I wouldn't dream of breaking that dear little man's heart," she whispered back. "Besides, I love Italian food."

"A girl after my own heart," he said lightly, his eyes holding hers longer than was necessary or wise, tearing his gaze away only to acknowledge the young woman who brought their wine.

"Do you eat here often?" Elisa asked once they found themselves alone again, feeling it was safer if their conversation returned to neutral territory. Somehow Luigi's did not fit into the picture she had formed of Garth. She helped herself to an anchovy and a bit of marinated artichoke and waited.

"Not as often as I would like to," the man conceded. "I've been coming to Luigi's for years—since I was an undergraduate engineering student at the university, and that's been a while. I like the place. It's more than the good food, it's the . . ." Garth paused, searching for the right word.

"The homey atmosphere?" Elisa speculated with interest.

"Perhaps that's it. I can relax here and forget everything. Very few of my business associates frequent Luigi's. I can be just another customer."

"I can't imagine you being just another anything," she commented with a shrug.

"Don't tell me that's a compliment coming from your lips?" He regarded her with good humor.

"I suppose it is in a way. You don't need me to tell you you're an attractive man," Elisa admitted cautiously. "No doubt dozens of women have said the same thing to you."

"Some."

"Were—are—you in love with Charlotte?" She was not sure where the question came from. She certainly had not intended to ask that of him.

The man frowned, folding his arms across his broad chest. "Oh, I see. Now we get down to the nitty-gritty."

81

He casually stretched his long legs under the table. "You might think better of me if I said yes, but the truth is I wasn't."

Thanks be to God! Elisa silently intoned, amazed by the sense of relief flooding through her. "I suppose we all just assumed—"

With a movement of his hand Garth brought her up short. "I can imagine what you all assumed. I wasn't totally blind to Charlotte's little game, you know." He gave Elisa a long look. "You knew?"

"I—I suspected. It was the self-satisfied way she talked about you one time, though she was hardly in the habit of confiding in me."

"I don't usually kiss and tell, but in this case I believe I will make an exception."

"No, really . . . you don't have to explain anything to me." Embarrassed, Elisa looked away. "Unless you want to, that is."

Garth sucked in his breath. "Charlotte and I did not go beyond the accepted proprieties, if that's what you're thinking. Not that she wasn't willing. Did she tell you we were sleeping together?"

The color rose in Elisa's face. "Not in so many words, but there were insinuations made. I didn't believe them," she hastily added.

"There was no reason why you shouldn't have," Garth said in a brisk tone, "unless you somehow realized that Charlotte could not accept rejection in any form. She's a very spoiled young woman used to getting her own way."

"I don't want to hear any more. It's really none of my business."

The man raised his eyes upward, indicating his need for patience. "*Now* she tells me! Honey, you could try the patience of a saint."

"And you're no saint, are you, Garth?" she stated with what suspiciously sounded like a muffled laugh.

82

"Are you toying with me, Miss Harrington?" he went on smoothly, his eyes sparkling green and brilliant.

"Just so you're not toying with me," the girl replied with quick pride.

"Never that, Elisa, you have my word." He seemed about to say more and then apparently changed his mind. "Ah, I see our lunch is here." Garth glanced up as the waitress returned with two heaping plates of lasagna.

"Hmm, it looks scrumptious!" exclaimed Elisa as she dove in. "I didn't think I would be hungry."

"Told you so," the man quipped. "Admit it, I was right."

"You were right . . . this once."

"I can see being engaged to you is definitely going to be a challenge, my dear Miss Harrington. By the way, I want to take you to the jeweler's after lunch to pick out a ring."

"A ring!" Elisa nearly choked on her wine. "Is that really necessary?"

"Of course. How else will the world and in particular one Chuck Stephenson know that you are out of circulation?"

"Considering we aren't going to stay engaged very long, isn't that a bit drastic, not to mention expensive?"

"I can afford it. You never know—we might like it."

"I really don't understand you sometimes, Garth Brandau," Elisa sighed, unconsciously straightening her back.

"Perhaps not, but what better way to get to know someone than as their fiancée?"

"Isn't that a little like putting the horse before the cart?"

"Look, Elisa, I know this whole thing between us has been cockeyed since last night."

"Since this morning," she corrected him.

"Since this morning, then, but I would like to get to know you better, to be your friend. Do you think we could begin again from there?" He was regarding her with serious intent.

The young woman put her hand in his. "Friends."

"Friends."

"Our lasagna is getting cold," Elisa finally said, breaking the spell.

"So it is." Garth disengaged himself gently, fully attentive to his meal now.

It was late afternoon when they returned to Elisa's apartment. The girl gazed down at the diamond sparkling on her left hand, thinking back to the moment when their eyes had lit upon this particular ring and then met in wordless assent. It was almost as if they were a young couple truly in love, choosing the time-honored symbol together. She had been stunned to learn the price—it wasn't a large stone—but once again Garth had brushed her objections aside with a word and a look. He had waited until they were alone in the Bentley before slipping the ring on her finger, briefly touching his lips to hers.

Elisa fumbled with the key to her apartment, sending the whole bunch noisily clattering to the hallway floor.

Garth bent down to retrieve them. "Here, let me do that," he said, sweeping her trembling hands aside.

"Would you like a cup of coffee or anything?" she politely asked once they were inside.

"No coffee, thanks, though you might interest me in the 'anything.'"

Pointedly ignoring the innuendo, Elisa stopped to pick up a piece of ragged notepaper from the coffee table. A frown creased her forehead as she read the note.

"Bad news?" queried her companion.

"No, it's from Brenda. I *think* it says she's working tonight and won't be in until late. Her handwriting is atrocious, you know."

"Then we have the place all to ourselves," the man murmured, coming up behind her and wrapping his arms around her waist. He nuzzled the side of her neck, sending goose bumps across her skin.

Elisa was intensely aware of Garth's vibrant form pressing against her. She felt her traitorous body melt in his embrace. "P-please, Garth . . ." He had kept such a comfortable, respectable distance all afternoon.

He swung her around to face him. "I know—'friends.' I'll try, Elisa, but it isn't going to be easy after this morning."

"I—I know. It isn't going to be easy for me either," she admitted.

Garth kissed her then, his tongue instantly asking that her mouth open beneath his, as it did. All reason vanished. All that remained for Elisa was this man who held her in his cast-iron arms and the havoc he could unleash with his kiss. Where was the neat and tidy Miss Harrington now? she asked herself.

"If I don't go now, Elisa, I may not be able to," he said, putting her away from him. "Will you have dinner with me tonight?"

She managed to nod her head.

"Be ready in two hours and wear something special."

"I-I'll be ready." She could not bring herself to look at him, lest he see in her eyes the very thing she preferred to keep hidden even from herself.

"I think we'll go to the busiest place I know. Being alone with you tonight would break a stronger man than I, Elisa Harrington. When you look like that, you could tempt the devil himself." With a surprisingly chaste kiss to her forehead the man made his timely exit.

"I'm afraid you are that devil, Garth Brandau," she whispered after his retreating form.

CHAPTER FIVE

"Damnation!" hissed the young woman as a dark smudge suddenly appeared beneath one eye. She plucked a tissue from the box on her dresser and gently wiped the mascara from her cheekbone.

What was the matter with her anyway? she muttered, out of patience with everything and everyone including herself. She was behaving like a flustered sixteen-year-old on her first date. Surely she had come farther than that in the intervening years, though she could scarcely deny the butterflies wreaking havoc in her stomach or the icy clamminess of her hands in spite of the balmy July evening.

Elisa threw down the mascara wand in disgust and pushed herself away from the dresser. Drastic situations called for drastic solutions. Without hesitation she marched to the liquor cabinet—actually no more than a shelf in the kitchen—and poured herself a generous portion of Scotch. She gulped the drink full strength, not bothering to add so much as an ice cube. The alcohol burned all the way down her throat, instantly spreading its warmth and calming her frayed nerves. She felt decidedly better as she returned to the bedroom to finish applying her makeup.

With one final stroke of the lipstick brush Elisa sat back to stare at herself in the mirror, nodding her head with satisfaction at what she saw there. A hand came up to gingerly caress the dark sweep of hair pulled back on each side of her face with an antique mother-of-pearl comb.

It was a more sophisticated style than she usually wore. Her customary shoulder-length flip seemed too casual for the evening ahead. Besides, by simply affecting a mask of sophistication she hoped to somehow find the necessary finesse to deal with a situation she wasn't the least bit certain she was up to.

As Elisa made to lower her hand it stopped in midair, the diamond on her finger catching the dying brilliance of the summer sunset. It sparkled like a thousand tiny slivers of light in the mirror. It was a beautiful ring, as near to perfection as Elisa had thought a thing could be. But beyond its cold stony beauty it gave her no pleasure.

The generous red mouth was drawn into a tight thin line of resolve. Elisa had battled with herself all evening, but her mind was made up now. She was determined that tonight she would return Garth's ring and dismiss him from her life. It was time to put an end to this ridiculous charade before the whole affair got out of hand. She couldn't possibly go through weeks or even days of a phony engagement to Garth Brandau. It had been madness to think she could. To go along with this crazy plan of his would only plunge her deeper into circumstances that were beyond her control. It was best to pull back now while she was still able to do so relatively unscathed.

Oh, but it had been a lovely day . . . lunching at that little Italian place with Garth . . . walking hand-in-hand through the shops. An afternoon in his company had been enjoyable as well as exhilarating, she thought wistfully.

Yet, there was a danger lurking just below the surface

that she couldn't quite put her finger on. She only knew it existed, it was real. Something warned Elisa not to allow herself to be caught up in the force of the man's personality. Garth Brandau did have more sex appeal in his little finger than most men had in their entire bodies and she might discover she was just as vulnerable as the next woman. Hadn't she, in fact, proved that this morning?

"You could make an awful fool of yourself if you're not careful," came the whispered entreaty, dark eyes meeting dark eyes in the mirror. "Face it, Elisa, you are attracted to him in a way that scares the hell out of you—as well it should if you've got any sense at all!" But then wasn't that normally the problem? One part common sense mixed with two parts physical passion did, indeed, make strange bedfellows—with good sense so often the loser.

Time to get a grip on herself, the girl chastised her reflection, feeling as though she had sleepwalked her way through the past day, not at all her usual self. A "stranger in a strange land." Well, both of her feet were back on old terra firma now and that was where they were going to stay!

Elisa stood up and walked across the bedroom to the closet. She was standing there in a white slip riffling through the half dozen or so decent dresses in her wardrobe when the doorbell sounded. It was precisely seven o'clock. Damn! The man *was* punctual.

Expediency made the choice for her in the end. Elisa tore the classic beige chiffon from its hanger and swiftly pulled it on over her head and zipped it. She slipped her feet into the one pair of Aigner dress sandals she owned, all straps and skinny heels as they were, on her way out of the bedroom.

"Coming!" she called out, stopping long enough to give her face and hair a final check in the bathroom mirror before answering the door.

It was Garth. He stood there smiling down at her,

heartbreakingly handsome in perfectly tailored brown trousers and a beige ultrasuede jacket. Elisa's breath caught in her throat for a moment, her heart pounding as if she were a teen-ager again and it was prom night to boot.

"I see we match," he observed, stepping inside at the girl's murmured invitation.

Elisa suddenly wished she had had a second helping of courage there in the kitchen.

"You look very lovely this evening." Garth leaned over and brushed her lips with his. "That dress suits you. I like to see a woman who knows what becomes her and dresses accordingly."

Or "undresses" accordingly, she thought crazily as his gaze seemed to take in every detail of her appearance from the fitted bodice, which Elisa knew emphasized her breasts, right down to the slender hips hinted at by the flowing skirt. She suddenly wished she had chosen a different outfit.

"W-why, thank you, sir." She nervously smiled back at him, her cheeks warmed by his scrutiny. "I'm afraid a graduate student's wardrobe is rather limited. Amanda and James seem to have an uncanny knack of supplementing mine at Christmas and my birthday. Thank goodness, my stepmother has excellent taste."

"I'd say she does," Garth said indulgently.

Elisa discovered she was twisting the diamond on her finger in agitated little movements. Oh, dear, had she been blabbering again?

"Would you like a drink before we go?" she inquired, almost hoping Garth would refuse the offer. Their liquor supply was pretty well limited to a six-pack of beer left over from moving day, the bargain-priced Scotch given to them as a housewarming gift that she had already sampled, and several bottles of undistinguished wine. Hardly the caliber of refreshments a man like Garth Brandau was no doubt accustomed to.

"Why don't we wait and have something at the club?" he suggested tactfully.

"All right, if you prefer." Elisa wondered if she sounded as relieved as she felt. "I'll just get my purse then," she added, retracing her steps to the bedroom. She retrieved the evening bag from her dresser and a matching chiffon scarf from the closet before rejoining Garth in the living room. "Shall we go?" She looked up at the man expectantly.

"Of course," he responded, taking her arm.

Elisa felt a little like Cinderella as she slid into the richly upholstered automobile. She leaned her head back and unconsciously let out a long sigh.

They had traveled several blocks in silence before Garth turned to study her profile. "You haven't asked where we are going," he commented, his attention once again diverted to the road ahead of him.

"No . . . I haven't."

"Lack of curiosity—how odd in a woman." The man appeared interested.

"Perhaps it's simply that I have the utmost confidence in your taste, which I'm sure is excellent."

"That's the second compliment you've given me today, Miss Harrington."

"Counting, Mr. Brandau?"

That brought an uproarious laugh from the man. "Best beware or you may even find yourself *liking* me." There was the slightest emphasis on his choice of verb.

"It's a chance I'll have to take, won't I?" Elisa smiled that secretive smile to herself that has driven men to madness since the Mona Lisa.

"I wish I knew what was going on in that pretty little head of yours," muttered Garth as he took the next corner rather too sharply. "Women are infuriating creatures."

"Funny, I was about to say the same thing about men." She felt pleased with the way she tossed that off.

90

The man's lips twitched in an effort not to smile. Good, thought Elisa, he was amused. Far better for both of them if the mood remained light and friendly and amusing. It was going to be a very long evening as it was.

"Would you like to listen to some music?" Garth politely inquired. At her affirmative nod he flipped a cartridge from the glove box and punched it into a concealed tape player in front of him. The raspy sounds of a French love song as only Charles Aznavour could sing it filled the spacious interior of the car.

Elisa tried not to appear surprised by his choice. She had scarcely thought of Garth as a romantic, except perhaps when it served his own purposes. She unconsciously straightened her shoulders, her brows drawing together in a thoughtful frown. Perhaps the "mood" music was intended for her benefit.

Good grief! The young woman moaned inwardly, her body slumping. She certainly did flatter herself. Why would Garth Brandau have the least bit of interest in putting her into any mood? If he did have any ulterior motive, which she seriously doubted, he was hardly the kind of man who needed to employ props. Elisa was quite sure he could attempt seduction and succeed strictly on his own merits.

It occurred to Elisa that Garth's car stereo must be the finest money could buy. It was as if she were center table at an intimate Paris cabaret. As the music enveloped her she sat back and tried to relax, translating the haunting lyric of the *chanson* in her head. The words burned into Elisa's mind, having a special significance for her on this night of all nights.

The song prompted the young woman to wonder once again if it wasn't wiser to follow the dictates of the heart in spite of the pain and misery it could bring than to let love pass one by. Love did seem to be everything to some people. Didn't one always take a chance when emotion was involved? After all, there were no guarantees for a broken heart.

Elisa Harrington did not often think of love or marriage. That was always for someday, not for now, not for her. What did she really know of love anyway? A few groping caresses of an overeager boyfriend when she was seventeen? The less-than-subtle passes of an amorous professor? The carefully controlled passion of a still-boyish Chuck Stephenson? Yet no one had tapped the inner core of passion she was herself only vaguely aware of. At least not until that morning when this man, who was virtually a stranger to her, had compelled Elisa to see her true nature.

For God's sakes, she was twenty-five years old today! Twenty-five! A quarter of a century. A third of a lifetime. And she knew so little of love or passion. And she had very nearly forgotten her own birthday. Elisa flicked away a stray tear that had come from nowhere to trace a path down her cheek. Silly goose, everybody was lonely sometimes.

"A penny for your thoughts," Garth said in his softest tone.

"A penny!" She faked the outrage. "Haven't you architects heard of inflation?" Elisa knew she must steer him away from any serious discussion. She couldn't handle it if Garth was going to be nice to her. "It will cost you at least a quarter," she teased.

"I—I don't think I have any change," the man said in all seriousness, one hand going to his trouser pocket.

"They weren't worth a quarter anyway," she said, trying to be flippant but failing.

Garth Brandau darted an odd look at her. Then without warning he pulled the Bentley to the side of the road and switched off the ignition. One hand lowered the volume of the tape player while the other took the girl's chin and turned her face toward his.

"Is there anything you would care to tell me, Elisa? You know what they say about a trouble shared."

"Yes, but no . . . I'm fine," she replied with dignity.

Garth exerted a subtle, almost imperceptible, pressure on her arm, pulling her closer still. "I see I have been remiss in my duties, Miss Harrington. There must be something that I can do to cheer you up." He spoke in riddles, but Elisa could well envision the form any "cheering up" would take when the man was Garth Brandau.

She suddenly realized, perhaps being totally honest with herself for the first time since she had found him in her apartment last night, that she wanted Garth to kiss her . . . not once but again and again. She nearly choked on her own rising passion. Where were all her good intentions now? Her heart began to pound furiously against her breast. Why didn't he do something? Say something? Surely he, too, must hear the gathering thunder that roared in her ears?

Disappointment sent her spirits crashing to the ground when, instead of taking her into his arms, the man reached across to the glove compartment and extracted a small velvet jeweler's box.

"I was planning to save this until later," he began by way of explanation, "but I think perhaps now is the time." Garth weighed his words carefully as he placed the box in her lap. "I hope you will consider this a memento of a very special day. At least it has been for me."

The young woman sat there staring at her hands. She realized that somewhere in this recital the music had stopped. She found it distracting that she could not place the exact moment the violins had fallen silent.

"Well, aren't you going to look at your present?" he prompted from close beside her, one arm sliding across the back of the seat as if he half expected her to bolt from the car.

"Y-yes, of course," stammered Elisa apologetically. She

said a quick fervent prayer that the approaching shadows of the evening would conceal her trembling from Garth's watchful eyes.

An involuntary sound escaped her as she opened the jeweler's box and beheld there against the black velvet a gold chain with a diamond heart at its center. Was her own heart such a fragile thing? she wondered.

"Oh, Garth." Only as she exhaled his name did Elisa realize she had been holding her breath. "It's—it's lovely, but I couldn't possibly—"

Garth put a restraining finger to her lips. A simple gesture but one that effectively halted the stream of objections they had both recognized as forthcoming.

"You can and you will. Please, Elisa."

Oh, God, how could she refuse him anything when he looked at her as he did now?

"But it's too much—" The word "money" trembled on her tongue and was rejected. How could she make this man—this man who had had money from the day of his birth—understand that no one had ever given her a gift even one-tenth the value of this necklace? After all, it was hardly a trinket. She couldn't help but wonder what in the world Garth gave a woman he was serious about if this was the kind of thing he handed out to someone he hardly knew.

The handsome man gazed intently into her eyes. "I do not make a habit of passing out diamonds as if they were candy, if that's what you're thinking. I want you to have it, Elisa. You are the only fiancée I've ever had, you know." His tanned face dissolved into a smile. "Cat got your tongue, my dear? Now, that is different."

"Thank you somehow seems so inadequate," Elisa brought out at last, choosing to ignore his comment.

"Believe me, it isn't," he hastened to reassure her.

"In that case, thank you, Garth," she said prettily. "It's the loveliest present anyone has ever given me. I—I'm a little overwhelmed." Elisa covered the short distance between them and touched her lips to his in a kiss as light as a butterfly. "And a special thank you for something you didn't even know: Today is my birthday."

"Your birthday!" the man echoed incredulously. "Why didn't you tell me?"

"I don't know," she began, not entirely truthful. "Yes, I do," she said, biting her lip. "I've always felt that going around telling everyone 'Hey, it's my birthday' was somehow like asking for presents. It makes me uncomfortable." Then she blushed. A hot, unstoppable blush right up to her ears.

"You mean you haven't told anyone it's your birthday?" he sought confirmation of the fact.

"No one but you, of course."

"And Amanda and James are hotfooting it around Europe after Charlotte."

"Yes, the last I heard," sighed Elisa.

"I am glad you told me," Garth murmured in her ear. "I think the 'birthday girl' deserves a kiss, don't you?"

"Deserves a kiss!" Elisa started to take offense but was brought up short by a smooth masculine jaw suddenly rubbing against hers, the tickling caress of his mustache as Garth's mouth followed the only recourse open to him making it impossible for her to speak at all.

It began as a gentle expression on her lips with only a hint of his earlier awareness of her as a woman. As Elisa's senses were heightened by the tantalizing scent of the man's cologne, the soft material of his jacket beneath her fingertips, the hard outline of his body pressing her back against the seat, she felt her defenses slipping away as if they were no more enduring than ashes in the wind.

Somewhere in the far back recesses of her mind it occurred to Elisa that she wanted Garth as she had never wanted another man. He had given her a taste of passion, now she wanted a second helping. As his kiss deepened,

95

drawing the last breath from her lungs, she gave herself up to the driving need that sprang to life beneath his caress.

As Garth went to move away it was Elisa who opened her mouth under his fading kiss, it was Elisa's tongue that took the first step in exploring the wonder of the man, though he quickly joined her in the exquisite search. When they finally broke apart, neither was breathing with complete normalcy.

"My God, I'd like to believe you don't respond like that to every man who kisses you!" Garth muttered huskily, his hands slipping from either side of her face to lightly encircle the slender neck.

The young woman interpreted the gesture not as a threat, but rather a caress, so gently did he hold her.

"I'm not going to tell you, Garth Brandau," she said, his passion giving her new courage. "A lady does have her secrets."

"I'd like to uncover all of your secrets," he continued in the same vein, nostrils flared, drops of perspiration dotting his forehead.

"That could take a lifetime," Elisa answered, unknowingly provocative.

"It might at that."

Something in his tone made Elisa glance at him, but the man's expression told her little.

"We'd better go," stated Garth in a rough tone, his hands dropping to his sides. "Our dinner reservation is for eight o'clock and it's nearly that now." A muscle in his jaw began to twitch as he quickly turned and started the automobile. "I don't know about you, honey, but I for one could use the distraction of bright lights and a lot of people around me. And I sure as hell need a drink!" He added the cryptic afterthought with a grimace.

Elisa closed her eyes and tried to calm the storm raging inside of her. The recent memory of Garth's caresses blotted out any rational thought. She felt like a fine instrument that had been tuned by the master only to be put aside while he pursued other pastimes.

"I—I could use a drink myself right now." She sat up straight, forcing a brightness into her voice she did not feel. "We'll toast my birthday. After all, it isn't every day a girl celebrates her twenty-fifth!"

It was a far more relaxed Elisa Harrington who three quarters of an hour later leaned across the white linen tablecloth to lightly touch her second glass of Dom Pérignon to Garth's.

"Hmm, this is delicious, and the view is magnificent," she enthused, looking out over Lake Mendota.

"I'm glad you approve of my choice." The furrows of tension had eased from around the man's eyes as well.

The young woman took a sip of her drink, noting the understated elegance of the club's dining room with its discreet lighting and tastefully arranged tables, the faint sounds of music in the background. It was both a public and a private place, though scarcely the bright lights and crowds of milling people Garth had intimated. Either way Elisa found herself relaxing in this atmosphere carefully calculated to do just that.

"Do you know who Dom Pérignon was?" Garth quizzed her, staring into the glass of sparkling wine he held at eye-level.

"I believe he was a French priest," said Elisa, not at all sure.

"That's one for you, Miss Harrington," he replied, a quickening look of interest in his green eyes as he regarded her over his glass. "He was indeed a Benedictine monk, cellarmaster at the abbey of Hautvillers, not far from Épernay, in the late seventeenth century. Historically, one theory that pertains to the development of champagne is that Dom Pérignon found a way to capture the bubbly effect that sometimes happened to the wine by chance. It supposedly took him twenty years to come up with a commercially feasible method."

"Right now I am very glad he did," giggled Elisa. "Let's drink a toast to the old boy."

"Perhaps we should order dinner," Garth proposed, discreetly signaling the waiter to approach their table.

"Yes, of course," Elisa said with deliberate sobriety. "I would like the sole amandine with asparagus, please." She honestly felt a fairly light meal would be all she could manage.

"I'll have the steak à la Milanese, asparagus hollandaise, baked potato, and a green salad," Garth followed with his own order.

"Yes, Mr. Brandau. Is there anything else I can get for you or the young lady, sir?"

"No, thank you. Wait! Yes, please bring us some of Henry's excellent stuffed mushrooms, Broadhurst." One glance at Elisa's slightly glazed eyes warned Garth that it might be wise to provide a little food as an accompaniment to the champagne.

With their order taken care of, the man's undivided attention reverted to his companion. Even in the dim lighting of the dining room, he could see she was literally bursting with curiosity. There was an unmistakable gleam in the brown eyes and a humorous tilt to her chin as she swayed toward him. She was undoubtedly amused by something he had said or done.

"All right, out with it, Elisa," came the command.

"How do you do it?"

Garth was genuinely puzzled by her question. "How do I do *what?*"

"How do you stay so—so—" Her eyes were drawn to the tapered waistline and lean abdomen evident beneath the fitted shirt. "How do you stay in such good physical shape when you eat like that all the time?" she asked as innocently as she could.

A deep, rich laugh shook his broad shoulders. "First, I do not eat like that 'all the time' and second—well, let's just say that my friends see to it that I get plenty of exercise." Then Garth laughed again.

Elisa felt her face burst into flames. She couldn't decide whether to join Garth in what he obviously considered a pretty amusing joke or pretend she hadn't heard him. She finally decided to ignore it altogether and abruptly changed the subject without the least attempt at subtlety, her third glass of champagne providing the necessary Dutch courage.

"Look here, Mr. Brandau"—she reverted to the formal address, feeling it would somehow make it easier to say what she had to say to him—"I think we need to discuss this supposed engagement of ours." Elisa glanced up at the man to see how he was taking it so far. He did not appear particularly pleased by the introduction of this subject into their conversation. A scowl creased his forehead, lending him an air of disapproval.

She was about to say more when Broadhurst suddenly reappeared at their table with a plate of delectably prepared mushroom caps. If she hadn't known better, Elisa would have suspected the waiter's timely intervention had somehow been choreographed by her escort.

"You will want to be sure to try these," Garth said smoothly. "They're one of Henry's specialties."

"Garth, we must talk!" she said with a touch of reproach.

"Of course, my dear, but I make it a rule never to discuss engagements on an empty stomach." His eyes crinkled up at the corners, all sign of his earlier displeasure gone.

"Garth! Garth Brandau!" A pretty thirtyish blonde had stopped several feet from their table. She was staring at them in delighted surprise. "Darling, look who's here!"

The woman impatiently tugged on the sleeve of the man beside her.

The man turned with a broad grin and held out his hand. "Garth!"

"Hello, Sally . . . Jeff." He nodded and rose to his feet to acknowledge their greeting.

"How are you anyway, you old devil?" The newcomer vigorously pumped Garth's hand, clasping one shoulder in a display of unmistakable affection. For an instant Elisa had an impression the two men were tempted to exchange a bear hug, so pleased were they to see each other.

"We haven't run into you in weeks, but now I think I understand why," said the man named Jeff, giving Elisa an appreciative wink.

Garth turned to her, his smile just the right mixture of possessiveness and endearment. "Darling, I would like you to meet two of my oldest and dearest friends, Sally and Jeff Cortland." The warning flashed by his darkened eyes was not missed by Elisa.

Biting down on the tip of her tongue, she swallowed the sharp retort that came to mind and tried to return the friendly smiles of the pair. Drat the man, he was doing it to her again! A good swift kick to the shin was what he deserved. Garth knew very well she had been about to call the whole thing off. She had the strangest feeling he was doing his best to foil her plan.

"And this is my fiancée, Elisa Harrington," he said, finishing the introductions almost offhandedly. Still, it didn't take a Philadelphia lawyer to see that the announcement was completely unexpected.

"Your fiancée? Aren't you the sly fox? Well, congratulations! We had no idea. . . ." The comments came in rapid succession.

It was Sally Cortland who finally got the situation in hand, her natural warmth and sincerity making themselves felt.

"You must forgive us, Miss Harrington. It's just that Jeff and I had no idea Garth had met someone. Not that we aren't delighted by the news, because we are. In fact, we're thrilled! Our best wishes to both of you."

"Thank you . . . but please, call me Elisa," the brunette heard herself respond, knowing as she spoke that her compliance in the matter meant the web of deceit was being woven all the tighter. She could hardly call Garth a liar in front of his friends. Even she wouldn't do that to the man. Not while she sat there with his ring on her finger.

"Shame on you for not telling us!" Sally scolded Garth good-naturedly.

"You are the first to know." He smoothed over the moment diplomatically. "I convinced Elisa to say yes to me just this morning."

Then he dared to look at her, the irony of the day's events written in his eyes. Elisa nearly choked. She put a hand to her mouth in a polite cough to cover her discomfiture.

"Are you all right, darling?" asked Garth solicitously.

"I'm fine, *darling,*" the girl ground through her teeth. "Something must have gone down the wrong way, that's all." She smiled at him with all the sweetness she could muster, knowing Garth would not be fooled.

"Then you two are celebrating your engagement tonight!" It finally dawned on Jeff Cortland.

"Yes," drawled his friend, "and it happens to be Elisa's birthday as well." -

"How terribly romantic—getting engaged on your birthday," sighed the other woman, exchanging glances with her husband that clearly bespoke the adoration they still shared.

"Why don't you two join us for a toast?" suggested Garth with what was perhaps surprising amiability.

"Oh, we shouldn't . . . you must want to be alone at a time like this." The Cortlands started to protest in unison.

"Please do, Garth and I would be delighted. Honestly we would." Elisa added her voice to his.

"Well . . . perhaps we could for just one drink, Jeff." Sally looked up at him expectantly. "We have nearly twenty minutes before we are supposed to meet the Chandlers for dinner and you know they are always late."

"True, and it isn't every day I get to toast a good friend's engagement," he rationalized.

With a practiced ease that displayed his organizational abilities, Garth Brandau had two additional glasses and a second bottle of Dom Pérignon delivered to their table as if it had been planned that way all along.

When the traditional toasts of happiness and best wishes were over, Jeff Cortland turned to the young woman on his right with what she was to discover was a habitual grin. "Where did you and Garth meet anyway? You aren't another one of those architects, are you?" he teased.

"Jeff is a lawyer, my dear, in case you didn't recognize the courtroom demeanor," Garth chimed in. "Don't let him disarm you with that boyish charm—he has one of the best legal minds in the business."

"He only says that because I'm his lawyer," Jeff said aside.

"Will you two please let the poor girl speak?" Sally joined in the free-for-all. "Are you an architect too, Elisa?"

"No, actually, I'm a graduate student in psychology." Even Elisa had to laugh at their reaction. It was one she was used to getting. "Garth and I first met at my parents' home through a mutual 'acquaintance.'" That was stretching the truth a bit, but she had always felt that an occasional white lie was essential to the continuance of human relations.

"Well, wherever or however you met is quite beside the point. We're just glad you did!" Sally added.

"You are going to be extremely popular with my friends, darling," Garth whispered to her, but so they all could hear. "Sally and Jeff have been trying to get me safely married off since I was best man at *their* wedding."

"Ten years ago this Christmas," the blonde supplied for Elisa's benefit.

The brunette's eyes grew wide with surprise. "Ten years!" It was out before she could exercise any prudence or form of self-censorship.

"Yes," laughed Sally, "here I am, having survived ten years, two houses, three children, a menagerie of cats, dogs, gerbils, and guppies that could put a pet store to shame, and working part-time." She spread her arms as if to encompass the lot.

"And you somehow do it all beautifully," said her husband with pride.

"I think it's darn right amazing!" Elisa eyed the woman beside her as if she were indeed amazing.

"Well, I can't take all the credit. Most women are not as fortunate as I am—professionally or personally. A good nurse can always work a few hours a week and I have a staunch supporter in Jeff. I don't know how women do it who work full-time outside the home though. Not if they have children."

"Most men don't want their wives gone all day everyday anyway," interrupted Garth. "I know I wouldn't want my wife to work."

"But how could you deny your wife the same satisfaction from a career that you assume is yours by some kind of natural right as a man?" Elisa could remain silent no longer.

"She would find her satisfaction in other ways," he said, very sure of himself.

Elisa sat there saying nothing. She was rather pale admittedly, except for a red spot in the center of each cheek, but she willed herself to show no other reaction to Garth's statement. After all, what was it to her if the man held nineteenth-century views in the twentieth century? The question was strictly academic anyway, and she refused to pick a fight with him under the circumstances.

As if they sensed the tension in the air, the Cortlands steered the conversation in a less controversial direction. Once the two men became involved in a discussion of their own, Sally sought to reassure the younger woman.

"I take it you and Garth haven't talked about your career."

"The subject never came up," she answered truthfully.

"I wouldn't worry, Elisa. When two people really love each other, they find a way to work these things out."

"Yes, I'm sure they do," the brunette responded at last. "Although I don't think even Garth could so easily dismiss the subject if he had had to work for his education as hard as I have for mine." Elisa could not disguise the anger that crept into her voice.

Sally studied her openly for a moment. "You know, you're different from the other women Garth has dated. For one thing you're interested in something besides Garth. I must confess the others were typically two-dimensional cutouts, all from the same mold. Only the name changed. I'm sure you know the type: blond, elegant, chic, but absolutely no character."

Yes, Elisa knew the type . . . all too well. The description fit Charlotte to a tee.

"In a way we were half afraid Garth might marry one of them and be miserable for the rest of his life. He's a brilliant man, at least about most things." Sally reached out for Elisa's hand and gave it a squeeze. "I'm so glad he didn't settle for second best, that he had the good sense to snatch you up. Garth will come around on the job thing, you'll see."

"Well, my sweet, while I do hate to break up the party,

104

it's time we were meeting the Chandlers and letting these two get on with their celebration," Jeff announced with a glance at his watch.

"Yes, I suppose so," acknowledged Sally, reluctantly getting to her feet. "Naturally we will want to have an engagement party for you. Just a few close friends . . ."

"Plans for a party can wait until next week, my love," he interrupted, putting an affectionate arm around his wife's shoulders.

"It was a pleasure meeting you, Elisa. I'll be in touch." Then Sally Cortland turned to Garth and placed a big kiss on his bronzed cheek. "We know you're going to be happy, dear friend. She's perfect for you."

"I—I like your friends. I like them very much," stammered Elisa once she found herself alone with Garth and not knowing what else to say.

"They obviously liked you as well."

"That makes two more people who know about our engagement," she sighed resignedly.

"Undoubtedly. I called my mother this afternoon after I left your place. She sends her love and asked me to tell you she's looking forward to meeting you very soon," Garth recited as if he had just thought of it.

"Your mother! B-but why?" Elisa's voice quivered with emotion.

"Why what?" he asked between bites of stuffed mushroom.

"Why, in God's name, did you have to go and tell your mother?"

"My mother lived in Madison for a good many years, Elisa. She still has a lot of friends here. Whatever we may feel about this engagement, I did not want her to hear of it through the grapevine," he explained, the faintest hint of scorn in his tone.

"Oh . . . I see." It seemed reasonable enough, she supposed.

"You were planning to call it off tonight before Sally and Jeff stopped, weren't you?" Garth's rigid posture dared her to contradict him. Elisa knew if she chose to do so he would have no compunction in pouncing on her as if she were the mouse and he the proverbial cat.

"Yes . . . yes, I was," she admitted, her voice so low, it was nearly inaudible.

"Would you care to tell me why? I thought only a few short hours ago we agreed it would be to our mutual benefit to keep it going for a while. Dammit, Elisa, I don't understand!" His handsome face was suffused with anger.

"I'm sorry, Garth. It was just that I wasn't sure I could keep up the charade. I'm not a very good actress." It was half of the truth anyway. But why was she apologizing to the man? He was as much to blame for the mess they found themselves in as she was. More so, in fact.

"Are you certain that's the only reason?" He was staring at her mouth as if he might like to slap her—or kiss her—silly. Thank goodness, neither was probable under the present circumstances.

Elisa's tongue nervously flitted across her lips in an effort to dispel their dryness. "Isn't that reason enough?" she demanded, refusing to meet his gaze straight on, afraid for herself, afraid, too, of what he might glimpse there in her eyes. "Oh, Garth, don't you see it would never work?"

"Why not?" he pressed.

She took a deep breath and began. "Because what happened between us this morning was something neither of us had any control over. I don't want to get involved in a casual affair with you or any man, Garth. Sex is not a game to me." The girl told him the truth, certain he would have hounded her until she did.

"It's called passion, sweety"—the endearment was a mockery—"and it has been known to rear its 'ugly' head between a man and a woman since it all started with Adam and Eve. I didn't see you objecting at the time. Without your roommate's untimely entrance, you would be mine now—body and soul!" Garth's anger took a cruel turn.

"Th-that's not true!" She hated him for saying it, all the while knowing it was true.

"Ah, come off it, Elisa. Who do you think you're kidding? I was there, remember? You wanted it as much as I did." He looked at her with cold contempt.

"That's the problem," she finally murmured in a husky voice, her hands twisting the linen napkin on her lap.

"Oh, for God's sake, you aren't a kid anymore and we weren't a couple of teen-agers necking in the backseat of a car. We're both consenting adults. If we want each other, there is no reason why we shouldn't make love."

"There is every reason in my book, Mr. Brandau. This will no doubt come as something of a surprise to you, but there are women who do not jump into bed with every *passably* attractive male who happens along," she stated, a shade haughtily.

They both realized it was a defensive measure on her part, but it did little to assuage Garth's anger. His face went gray. His eyes were two narrow slits as he glared across the table at her.

No doubt she had wounded his fragile male ego, Elisa scoffed with uncharacteristic cynicism.

Then something happened to the man. She had no explanation for it, but some emotion she had not seen there before flickered behind his eyes. It was like a light going on in a dark room.

"You—you wouldn't be trying to tell me in your own roundabout way that you have never slept with a man, would you?" The sideways glance Garth gave her was disconcertingly shrewd.

"While *you* may be accustomed to waking up with someone in your bed who for all practical purposes is a stranger, I am not!" Elisa sniffed indignantly.

"My God, it's true, then?" There was no mistaking the amazement in his voice.

The color rose in the girl's face like a flag, unwittingly giving him his answer.

Garth Brandau put his head back and let out a whoop. "It is true! Why didn't you tell me?" The man's face broke into a broad grin suspiciously akin to triumph.

"Are you making fun of me, Garth?" she demanded with a real sense of injury, her dark eyes shooting daggers at her tormentor. He *was* making fun of her and it was hurtful, terribly hurtful. Elisa Harrington was dismayed to find that his opinion meant more than even she had suspected.

The man immediately reached out to reassure her. "No, Elisa, never that, believe me." His voice was very gentle. "There were a few things I couldn't figure out before, that's all." Garth did not expound. Then he smiled at her, unleashing the full impact of his charm, a charm she was sure men and women alike found irresistible. "I'm sorry if I sounded angry earlier. This is your birthday and I wouldn't do anything to spoil that for you. Let's put the past few minutes behind us and start again with our celebration. What do you say, honey—shall we paint the town?"

Elisa found this simple inquiry unexpectedly difficult to answer. She knew somehow, in a vague, wine-induced sort of way, that the choice she made now would have far-reaching effects for her. If she insisted, Garth would take her home this very minute.

Here she was being careful and cautious all over again. And where had prudence ever got her? What the hell! This was her twenty-fifth birthday and she was out with the most attractive man she had ever met. It was indeed now or never.

Unsteadily Elisa's heart began to pick up speed. "Could I please have another glass of champagne, Garth?" Her best and brightest smile was bestowed upon the waiting man.

CHAPTER SIX

As Garth Brandau leaned over and pressed a chaste kiss on the girl's forehead, even he must have considered his behavior a little out of character. His lips lingered there for a moment against her silky smooth skin. It was warm, smelling of sweet wine and a light flowery scent.

Then he pulled back and took the latchkey from Elisa's outstretched hand and unlocked the apartment door, gallantly standing aside so she could enter.

"I'll give you a call in the morning, but not too early . . . I promise," he said with a wry smile, as if to take his leave.

He watched as Elisa's face changed with startling suddenness, her mouth turning down at the corners.

"You aren't coming in?" she inquired, unable to disguise her disappointment.

Garth took in a long breath, putting his hand on her shoulder with apparent casualness. "I don't think it would be a good idea, honey."

"Can't you come in for a few minutes anyway? I could fix us a drink or something if you like. Brenda isn't home yet," she stated with certainty, although it was beyond him how she could possibly know that for a fact.

"I'm sure your roommate will be back at any time," he reassured her, sensing she did not wish to be on her own.

"No, she won't," Elisa pouted, rather in the manner of a sulky child. "She said in her note that it would be late." She tugged on his arm as if she thought herself capable of moving the stonelike figure.

"It is one thirty now, Elisa," he pointed out to her.

"That's not very late, at least not for Brenda. Sometimes she doesn't get off work until two or two thirty."

The young woman turned a pirouette into the middle of the rather threadbare living room, dislodging one of the mother-of-pearl combs in the process. It dropped soundlessly to the carpet, there to be retrieved by Garth, who had followed her into the apartment despite his good intentions to the contrary.

"I haven't thanked you yet for the wonderful evening," she sighed, her voice a dreamy song on a summer's eve.

"I'm sure you will think of some appropriate gesture," he muttered under his breath.

"Hum? Oh, Garth, the food was wonderful. The champagne was wonderful. Even you were wonderful. It might not be so bad being engaged to you—temporarily, of course." Elisa bit down on her lip, realizing, perhaps too late, that the wine had loosened her tongue.

She looked up at him and discovered he was staring at her. For a moment she even thought she glimpsed a hunger in his eyes that mirrored her own feelings, but only for a moment. Then a shutter snapped back into place.

"Would you like something?"

"Elisa . . ." Her name seemed to be dragged from Garth against his will.

She felt herself drawn across the room toward him. She came to a full stop directly in front of the man and waited.

111

When it became apparent he was not going to make the first move, Elisa took the initiative.

"Aren't you going to kiss your fiancée good night, Mr. Brandau?" It was bold of her to ask, far and away the boldest thing she had ever done. The proof was in her heart slamming against her chest. "You haven't come near me all evening, except that once in the car, of course, and when we were dancing," she reminded him quite unnecessarily, her arms reaching up to entwine themselves about his neck in a reenactment of their dance posture. "Would you like to dance now? I could always hum us a song." With that Elisa began to sway against him, softly singing to herself.

"Behave yourself!" the man growled in a soft voice, but she noticed he made no attempt to extricate himself.

"I don't want to behave myself." A little frown formed on her lips. "Where's the fun in being Miss Goody-Two-Shoes all the time?"

"You, my dear Miss Harrington, do not hold your liquor well. I can see now I shouldn't have allowed you that last glass of champagne," Garth scolded indulgently, brushing a stray curl back from her face as he dropped a light kiss on the tip of her nose.

"Am I to believe, then, that this is an example of the fatal Brandau charm of which I've heard so much? Or do you bid all of your women good night with a peck on the nose?" she teased, running her hand down the front of his shirt and back up again until it slipped inside next to his skin.

"Don't try your female wiles out on me, Elisa. You have a lot to learn, but I am not going to be the one to teach you. You don't know what you're asking for, and I suspect you've had too much to drink besides," he said in a hard, dry voice.

"I do know, and I'm not the least bit tipsy," she insisted. "Why don't you kiss me, since it's obvious you aren't in the mood to dance?" She knew it was provocative of her, but Elisa found the experience of touching a man—or at least this man with his smooth skin and granite-hard muscles—enjoyable beyond anything she had imagined. One button of his shirt came undone, granting her even greater freedom in her explorations. The masculine aroma of him was like another glass of champagne to her senses, pleasurable and intoxicating.

"If I do kiss you good night, will you be a good girl and run along to bed?" He conceded one point, hoping to gain another.

Elisa's eyes were wide and full of innocence. "Of course, Garth," she boldly lied.

Seemingly in slow motion the man's face drew near. When his kiss came, it was a tribute to Garth's self-control. He touched his lips to her mouth, her eyes, the tender spot where neck and shoulder met. Only the acceleration of his heartbeat beneath her hand gave him away. He was not so immune as he would have her believe. It was a satisfying thought.

After a few seconds he drew away sharply. Elisa took a deep breath, her tongue making nervous little forays to her lips.

"Is that the best the great Garth Brandau can do?" she chided, her arms retaining their position around his neck though Garth's had fallen to his sides.

"Dammit, Elisa, don't push me!"

"What are you so upset about? I'm only asking for a decent kiss." The man stiffened, giving her a long measuring look. "Oh, relax, Garth," she exclaimed with a laugh. "What could it hurt?"

"Offhand I can think of any number of things," he said, without a trace of humor.

"Surely you aren't afraid, are you?" The young woman pushed him hard, the challenge clearly there in her teasing manner and sparkling eyes.

113

Garth's lips compressed into a tight line; anger flashed momentarily in the vivid green eyes. "No, I'm not afraid, but perhaps you should be. You told me earlier that you didn't play games. Remember? Well, I don't either, honey. But if I did, we would have one hell of a time establishing the ground rules. You shouldn't go around picking on men with twice your experience, Elisa. That's rule number one."

Elisa's nerve crumpled along with her face. "Dammit, Garth, I am not a child! I'm twenty-five."

"I know that." He ran his eyes over her.

"I am twenty-five years old," she repeated louder, as if he hadn't heard her. Elisa closed her eyes and made herself say the words. "Do—do you think I'm pretty?"

"I think you're beautiful." His voice sounded odd. "You aren't thinking anything silly like 'Since I'm a twenty-five-year-old virgin, there must be something wrong with me,' are you?" He gave Elisa that shrewd, narrow stare again.

The color rose sharply in her young face. "Well . . ."

"Ah, c'mon, honey, how many men have tried to get you into bed with them?" The question was meant to boost her sagging ego.

Elisa modestly cast her eyes down. "Lots, I suppose," she replied without thinking.

Once he had his answer, Garth Brandau found he did not care for it one bit. "Are—are you sure not even one of them succeeded?" His fingers tightened on her upper arms.

She tried, however unsuccessfully, to shake off his hold on her. "Now, that is a silly question. It's hardly the kind of thing a girl would be mistaken about, is it?"

"Then why were you willing to let me make love to you this morning?"

Dark, confused eyes came up to meet his. "I don't know

why." She made a slight gesture with her hands. "It wasn't so much a matter of letting you make love to me, it was just something that happened between us."

"You're right, it is this thing that happens between us," Garth assented on a harsh breath, his mouth moving along her cheek to the tip of a small pink ear. He caught it gently between his teeth. "I can feel you tremble in my arms whenever I touch you. Do you have any idea what that does to me, little girl?"

"N-no," she replied, her voice vibrating slightly. But she did know. That morning she had felt the blood pounding in his veins, his heart racing beneath her hand, as it was even now.

Garth groaned something Elisa could not make out as he finally complied with her wishes. His mouth overwhelmed her. Then the kiss began to tease, to taunt her until she thought she would surely go mad with the sensations it created. Garth's hands found the long length of her, then up the side of her body to skirt the rounded swell of her breast. There was no denying the hard peak that rose to meet his touch through the layers of clothing.

As one who needs a long deep draft of water, not merely a few drops, Elisa tried to find his mouth in a satisfying kiss. "Please, Garth, I—I can't take much more of this," came the frenzied whisper.

"Sweet torture, my love. Neither can I," he breathed heavily, giving her of himself without reserve at last.

Elisa Harrington had never been kissed so thoroughly in all her life. She had wanted this man to kiss her silly, to caress her as only he had done, to love her as a man loves a woman—and that was exactly what he was doing.

Without a word Garth gathered her up in his arms and headed for the nearest chair. When he sat down, Elisa found herself on his lap. Gone was any hesitancy, any reluctance he may have felt. Urgency ruled his actions now, his mouth ready and willing to resume the lesson where they had left off. And with Garth as her teacher, Elisa was indeed an eager student.

When he kissed her, the world stood still for a moment. He drew the life from her until she wanted nothing more than to die there in his arms. One hand captured the girl by the chin while the other molded her to his liking. Elisa was intensely aware of the vibrant body pressing against her. An insistent thumb stroked her lips until they parted to his probing tongue.

The man's expert manipulation located the zipper that ran its course down the back of her dress. His agile fingers tested its workings. The chiffon slipped away from her shoulders as his mouth sought out and found each point where Elisa's pulse raced in time to his. She felt as if Garth's brand was burned onto her flesh with every caress. Then the straps of her slip and bra were effortlessly put aside, freeing the two milky globes from their lacy imprisonment.

"God, you're perfect!" muttered Garth, sounding as though his mouth were filled with cotton.

Elisa sucked in her breath as a finger lazily traced the outline of her breast, the nipple forming a rosy bud ripe for the picking. Conscious of the deep green eyes taking in every inch of her exposed skin, she tried to cover herself.

"No, don't! Don't, Elisa." He halted her fidgeting. "You have a beautiful body. Any man would gladly lose himself in its sweetness." He ended on a tortured groan, his mouth seemingly compelled to taste the forbidden fruit.

Wild desire flooded her being as Elisa had never known before. Her hands began their own frantic search, unbuttoning Garth's shirt so her bare breasts could be crushed against the mat of masculine skin and hair. Their bodies met in an explosion of sensuous longing that neither could deny, nor did they wish to.

She pressed a fevered kiss to the spot above his heart, her tongue flickering across his male nipples. She took in the smell and the taste of the man as if he were life's sustenance to her starved senses.

A burst of profanity came from Garth as he jerked away. "Where did you learn to do things like that?" he spoke hurriedly, almost harshly.

"I—I just thought since you did it to me—Wasn't it all right?" She was still shaking with reaction, suddenly looking very young and unsure of herself.

Garth gave a tired laugh and pulled her back into the circle of his arms. "Yes, it's all right. Damn!" he swore, resting his chin on her damp forehead. "It's more than just all right. The real problem is what am I going to do about you, little girl?" He seemed to be waging some kind of war with himself. "A virgin of any age, whether she be eighteen or eighty, is hardly my style. Yet I would gladly beat to a bloody pulp any man who dared to touch you as I have. Kissing you, touching you like this—it isn't enough for me, Elisa."

"I know," she managed to get out, choked by emotions she could not express.

"I wonder if you do," he said skeptically.

"I'm not a child, Garth."

He moved restlessly. "Look, sweetheart, I want nothing less from you than to have you in my bed, all warm and yielding. To caress you, to bring to life again all that passion stored up inside you." His words seduced her when only minutes before it had been his kisses.

"I want you too," murmured Elisa, her face buried in his shirt. "What are we going to do about it?" she finally asked in a small voice.

Garth gripped her fingers so tightly, she winced. "We can't do a damn thing about it. At least not now, not tonight." He tipped her chin back. "I know what I'm talking about, Elisa, so don't look at me like that. When

117

you make love for the first time, it should be perfect. Not like this . . . in the wee hours of the morning when you've had too much champagne the night before and your room-mate is due home any minute. And I suspect in the clear light of day you may see it all differently," he commented with a degree of worldliness she did not possess.

"No, I won't, you know," she murmured, her fingers toying with his shirt button.

"Then you stand forewarned, Miss Elisa Harrington, because common sense may not always win out over what you do to me. I'm thirty-five years old, Elisa, and I should know better, but I want you. I want you so badly, it's like a knife twisting in my gut. Only you can put me out of my misery."

A quiver ran down the back of her neck as he spoke, like a vial of quicksilver. In one form or another, since Elisa was sixteen, men had expressed a desire for her . . . but never in quite so elemental terms. The veneer of niceties was swept aside by this man who cared little for them when they did not serve his purposes. Not that she had any reason to doubt what Garth said. In fact, she believed every word.

"C'mon, honey, we better put ourselves to rights before Brenda walks in on us again." An ironic smile touched his lips.

Yet it was with a gentleness she had not known he possessed that the man fixed her dress and stood her back on her feet. "Thank you," she said, suddenly all cool politeness, trying to scrape together the tattered shreds of her dignity.

"Anytime, ma'am," Garth mocked her just a little. Then he leisurely got up from the chair and went about the task of straightening his own clothing, apparently fully recovered from the episode that had taken place between them.

Ready to take his leave, he came up to her and dropped

118

a hard swift kiss on the girl's mouth. "Now off to bed with you while my better instincts still have the upper hand," he ordered with a patronizing slap to her backside.

So he thought he called all of the shots, did he? Sometimes Garth was a bit too arrogant for her liking. "I might say the same to you," Elisa returned spiritedly. "Sweet dreams!"

"I doubt it," he grumbled. "Since it is highly unlikely that I will get any sleep at all tonight."

"In that case, would you care to borrow the book I'm reading? I'm quite sure I won't be needing it." She executed a polite yawn behind her hand. "Perhaps it will help take your mind off your problems," she said sympathetically, taking the book from a shelf behind her and placing it in his hands.

Garth read the title aloud, *"The Joy of Sex?"*

"Ah, you've read it." It was Elisa's turn to rib him a little.

"Very funny, Elisa, very funny." He obviously did not find it so.

"Well, if that doesn't do the trick, I've heard a cold shower sometimes helps."

The look he gave her said it all. "Good night, Elisa."

"Good night, Garth, and—ah—happy sailing!" She quickly closed the door after him while the last word was still hers.

She was standing under the undulating spray of hot water, wishing her head belonged to someone else, when the familiar voice of Brenda Collins penetrated the steamy haze.

"Are you all right, Elisa? You've been in there for nearly a half hour."

Elisa forced a civility into her voice that she was far from feeling. "I was washing my hair," she called out, as if that somehow explained everything. "Oh, Brenda, I've

119

forgotten my towel." She peeked around the edge of the shower curtain. "Would you be a dear and hand it to me?" Elisa indicated the bathsheet on the edge of the sink.

With her hair turbaned in a smaller towel and the larger secured sarong-style around her body, Elisa carefully stepped from the shower. "Oh . . ." She put a hand to her head.

Brenda bit the corners of her mouth against a smile. "A little too much celebrating last night?"

"Dom Pérignon 1973. I had four—no, five glasses. Or was it six?"

"Well, at least you went in style," observed her roommate. "I've never had a classy hangover. I wonder if it feels any different from the beer-and-pretzels variety."

"I think the question is purely academic. I feel wretched! And don't make me laugh, Brenda, that would be cruel and unjust punishment in my present condition," groaned Elisa.

"Are you seeing him today?"

"Garth said he would call this morning. What time is it anyway?"

"After eleven."

"Oh, I'm not ready to face this day yet." She plopped down on the edge of the tub. "How could something that felt so good last night feel so bad this morning?"

"That's what we all ask ourselves. My dear Lisa, I may be younger than you are in years, but I'm so much older in experience," said her roommate with genuine fondness.

"Now don't *you* start on me, Brenda Collins! I have had enough of that from Garth Brandau." Her lips folded in that soft, obstinate line.

"He is quite a bit older," Brenda said with a shrug.

"Ten years doesn't mean a hill of beans when the woman is twenty-five and the man thirty-five." She sounded more than doubtful.

"It might if you're the woman and the man is someone

120

like your Garth Brandau," Brenda commented in all seriousness. "I've seen men like that in action. I just don't want to see you get hurt."

"I know." Elisa's voice was a husky whisper.

"Are you sure you know what you're doing, sweety?"

"No," the young woman admitted with a ragged laugh. "Please, no lectures, Brenda. We all have to grow up sometime, even we late bloomers."

"Yes, but to cut your milk teeth on a man like that. You're either very brave or crazy," Brenda said, shaking her head. "C'mon, I'll dry your hair for you. You don't appear to be moving too fast this morning."

She took out the blow dryer and assorted paraphernalia and issued her instructions. "You sit there and relax. I'll have your hair looking terrific in a jiffy. Your eyes don't look so good though," she added after the briefest of pauses.

"You should see them from this side," Elisa muttered dryly, her left hand going up to shade her eyes. "Boy, it seems bright in here."

"It's probably the reflection from that rock you're wearing," Brenda said, pursing her lips. "Oh, but it is a beautiful ring, don't get me wrong."

"Yes, it is," replied Elisa, looking somewhat uncomfortable. "But it isn't all that big. I mean, there were larger stones Garth wanted me to consider."

"If the man has that kind of money to spend, and I'm sure he has, then why not choose the best?" She mellowed, trying to be conciliatory. By mentioning the size of the diamond, Brenda realized she had hit a raw nerve. She hadn't meant anything by it. "*Voilà!*" she exclaimed as she finished performing her magic. "If I do say so myself, you look one hundred percent better."

Elisa gave her friend a little hug. "Thank you. I feel better too."

"I'll go make some fresh coffee—" Brenda was interrupted by the sound of the doorbell. "Are you expecting anyone?"

"No."

"Perhaps Garth decided to come over instead of calling."

"I hope not, but just in case, would you answer it? I'll slip into my room and throw on a pair of jeans."

"Sure."

The two parted company in the hallway. Within the privacy of her bedroom Elisa threw off the towel and quickly dressed in her oldest jeans and a T-shirt that had seen its share of laundering.

She stopped to look at herself in the mirror, grateful there were no outward signs of the previous night's overindulgence beyond a slightly strained expression around the eyes. She picked up a tube of lipstick and ran the nearly colorless gloss across her mouth. Her one concession to the possibility it might be Garth Brandau at the door was a dab of perfume behind each ear and at the base of her throat. Some perverse streak of stubbornness made her take no further steps to enhance her appearance. Though Elisa was the only one blind to how fresh and unaffected and downright sexy she looked in the tight jeans and clinging shirt.

"Elisa . . ." A sibilant hiss came from the doorway. "It's Garth. I've left him in the living room. Are you dressed?"

"Yes, I'll be right out. Thanks, Brenda," she replied.

Despite her resolve to remain cool and calm, Elisa's heart was drumming like a timpani as she came forward to greet her caller.

"Good morning, darling." Garth covered the remaining distance between them at a leisurely gait. "How are you feeling this morning?" he grinned, a boy's grin, as he lowered his head for the obligatory kiss.

The girl received it with as much grace as she could muster under the circumstances. "Don't you dare be cheerful, Garth Brandau. I will gladly strangle you if you dare to be cheerful!"

"Feeling a little under the weather, my love?" His eyes were laughing.

"I'm fine, thank you." She met his gaze with a challenging lift of her chin.

"I thought you might have found our celebration last night too much for you." His laugh was excellently done.

"Not at all."

"I've brought you a present anyway," he said, extracting a thermos from the sack she now saw he held in his hand. "It's an old family recipe passed down from father to son: Aunt Lydia's Home Remedy—guaranteed to cure whatever ails you, especially if it's a hangover."

Elisa held up one hand in front of her as if to fend off his approach. "Thanks but no thanks."

"Now, honey, I know what's best for you, at least in this case. You do as you're told. You know what happens to little girls who don't listen to their elders?"

A muffled snicker from behind the couple alerted them to Brenda's continued presence in the room.

"Don't you have something requiring your attention somewhere else, Miss Collins?" Garth suggested autocratically.

"Yes, sir! I nearly forgot. It's my turn to polish the silver." She cast a mischievous grin in their direction, then disappeared around the corner. "I'll be in my room if you need me, Elisa."

"She won't," Garth tossed over his shoulder at the retreating form of the woman. Then his attention immediately reverted to Elisa. She had noticed before the way he had of making a woman feel as if she were the only thing in the world that interested him, that everyone and everything else ceased to exist at that moment. It was a heady sensation. "You just make yourself comfortable, honey,

123

while I go out to the kitchen and stir up a healthy dose of Aunt Lydia's cure-all for you."

"Oh, all right," she said rather ungraciously. Elisa had discovered it was sometimes wiser to give in than to argue with the man. And he certainly seemed in fine spirits this morning, apparently suffering none of the aftereffects she was.

"Don't miss me too much while I'm gone," he teased, giving her a kiss that she couldn't have forgotten if she tried. She was rather breathless when Garth finally let her go. He looked her straight in the eye, his gaze unwavering. "I thought perhaps it was the champagne or the summer night, but it wasn't." Then he disappeared into the kitchen, leaving Elisa staring after him, her mouth agape.

No sooner had he gone when the doorbell rang again. Opening the apartment door, she was utterly taken aback to see the tall, broad figure of Chuck Stephenson.

"Hi, Elisa!" he grinned unsuspectingly, giving her a big kiss on the cheek. "I got back early and came over to see if you're free this afternoon. I thought we might go to a movie or out to the lake."

Elisa took a step backward. "H-hello, Chuck." Oh, Lord, this was all happening too quickly. She wasn't ready for it. The throbbing in her head began anew, and the hand she pressed to her temple found it hot to the touch. The enormity of the changes she had allowed to take place in her life in the past two days hit Elisa like a slap across the face. Rather guiltily she realized she had not once thought of Chuck during the last twenty-four hours.

"I wish you'd changed your mind about coming home with me. It wasn't much fun without you."

"It was for the best, Chuck, believe me," she said in a low, earnest tone as she lowered her gaze.

When he did not respond, Elisa finally ventured a look at the man in front of her. There was no mistaking what was written on his handsome features—shock, disbelief, anger—they were all there.

"What the hell! Is that what I think it is?"

It took her a moment to realize he was referring to the ring she wore. There was no sense lying to him. She may as well get it over with.

"Yes, it is," her voice rasped.

Chuck did an abrupt about-face and stalked toward the door.

"Please, Chuck, at least let me try to explain. We've been friends for a long time. I don't want it to end like this." She struggled to express herself.

A bitter laugh shook his broad shoulders. "Friends, Elisa? Was that all I ever meant to you?"

"Oh, Chuck, I'm sorry."

A look of cold fury came over his face. "I don't know what you could possibly say that would make any difference." He was hurt and it showed.

Elisa looked wildly around her. "It's rather difficult to explain."

"I'll bet it is." She was surprised at the bitterness in his voice. "Oh, honey, why did you do it? And behind my back like this." The young man reached out for her, but she just as determinedly evaded his grasp. "Dammit, Elisa, you knew how I felt about you!"

She wryly noted his ready use of the past tense when referring to his undying devotion. It hardened her heart just a little. Not that she blamed Chuck, but the depth of his affection, an affection she seemed to have taken for granted, certainly came into question. Here she had thought for some time now that their relationship hadn't progressed beyond the comfortable dating stage because she wasn't ready or willing. Now she wasn't so sure that was the only reason.

"Sometimes these things happen," she said dryly, suddenly feeling she may have outgrown Chuck and not even realized it.

"Is it anyone I know?" He raked a hand through the unruly mop of blond hair.

"You might, but I don't think so." She concentrated on her upturned palms. "His name is Garth Brandau." She said it quickly, praying that the man in question would not show his face.

Chuck Stephenson looked at her like she was crazy. "Garth Brandau! You can't mean that rich playboy? The one who's an architect?" He put his head back and crowed like a rooster.

"Garth is an architect and yes, I believe he may be rich, but he most certainly is not a playboy!" she heard herself hotly defend him.

"Come on, Elisa, you've had your fun. Now where did you really get that ring? I must say it almost looks real."

She shook off his hand angrily. "It is real and I am engaged to Garth Brandau."

Chuck still did not believe her, that much was obvious. Elisa could see it in the curl of his lip, not altogether an attractive gesture on his part.

"What the hell would a man like Brandau want with you? He could have his pick of the crop and I've heard he likes his women to be just that—women." He chuckled in rather an offensive way.

Elisa's face first went fire-engine red and then lost all color. She had never heard Chuck talk like this. Somehow his boyish manner seemed crude, his size awkward, even oafish.

"Elisa, honey, your drink is ready." The rich timbre of Garth's voice coming from the hallway behind them heralded his arrival on the scene. In an instant he was there beside her, a possessive arm curled around her waist. "Aren't you going to introduce your *friend,* darling?" His voice was easy, but his relaxed stance was a quiet threat.

"Of—of course, darling." She took her cue from him. "This is Chuck Stephenson, a friend from the university. Chuck, this is my fiancé, Garth Brandau."

"I've heard of you, naturally, Mr. Brandau," mumbled Chuck, as he accepted the hand extended to him. Although Chuck was the taller of the two men by a good three or four inches, there was no doubt in any of their minds who dominated the situation.

"It's always a pleasure meeting one of Elisa's old friends," Garth said smoothly.

"Well, actually, Elisa and I were more than just friends at one time," Chuck went on with a self-conscious laugh.

"I know all about your 'friendship' with my fiancée, Stephenson," he replied, ignoring the implication.

"Yes, well, I have to be running along. I just stopped by to ask Elisa a question about one of her classes," the younger man said somewhat lamely.

"And did you give Chuck his answer, honey?" It was impossible to tell whether or not Garth spoke ironically.

"I'm sure Chuck understands perfectly," she said, measuring out her words.

"It was—ah—nice meeting you, Mr. Brandau." He backed off toward the door. His eyes, indifferent rather than hostile, touched Elisa's briefly. "See you around sometime." Then he was gone as suddenly as he had appeared.

With an exaggerated sigh of relief Elisa sank down into one of the chairs. "Whew, I'm glad that's over with! I thought for a moment there he might get nasty. Thank you for coming to my rescue."

"Anytime, ma'am. That's what we knights on white chargers are for. Now for Aunt Lydia's cure . . ."

The young woman clasped the mug between her hands and took a sniff. "Ugh! Is this one of those times when the cure is worse than what's ailing you?"

"Don't let the aroma put you off. I guarantee you'll feel better in no time if you drink it all down."

"I guess I'll have to take your word for it," she said guardedly.

"Have you eaten yet?"

Elisa gave him a dirty look over the top of the mug. "You've got to be kidding!"

"I know a great little restaurant not far from here that serves the best omelets in Madison."

"Oh, Garth, I can't. I have to study this afternoon and I'm scheduled to work the evening shift at the library."

"Couldn't you call in sick?" the man asked, as if that was precisely what he expected her to do.

"No, I couldn't," Elisa stated in a quiet, determined voice. "Miss Haskell is counting on me and I need the money."

"And who, pray tell, is Miss Haskell?"

"The head librarian."

"I see." Garth took a small leather appointment book from his coat pocket and flipped through several pages. "I have Wednesday evening open. Would you like to have dinner with me?"

Elisa was already shaking her head. "Can't. I work at the mental health clinic every Wednesday."

"Then what about Friday?" he asked, piqued. "No, I can't. I have a dinner meeting. Damn! I can't get out of that one either. I'm the keynote speaker."

"I'm free for a few hours on Thursday. We could have lunch."

"I'll be in Milwaukee on Thursday." Garth snapped the book closed and returned it to his pocket.

"Oh." Elisa bit her lip thoughtfully.

"I don't believe this. We can't manage even one hour together in the next week?" He was half laughing and half angry. "I've never run into this problem before. What is it with you anyway, Elisa?"

So, male chauvinism was going to rear its ugly head after all. The young woman flung up a defiant chin. "Perhaps it's because you're used to women being at your beck and call. Well, I happen to have a life of my own, Garth, and I won't give it up for any man. I cannot drop everything just to wait around here for you to telephone or drop by."

Garth gave her a funny look. "That much seems obvious."

"I—I don't have to work next weekend," she said, softening. "We could go on a picnic."

Garth studied her for a moment. "All right, Saturday morning. Ten o'clock. I'll pick you up," he stated gruffly. "And I'll supply the lunch."

Elisa visibly brightened. "Saturday it is, then."

When he stood to go a few minutes later, Garth drew her into his arms and kissed her long and hard. "Oh, God, and that is supposed to last me a whole week!" he growled in a husky voice.

"I'm sorry," she whispered weakly.

"You're not half as sorry as I am, Elisa Harrington. It's going to be one hell of a long week!"

For one wild, crazy moment Elisa almost called him back, ready to cancel everything, wanting to be with him more than anything else in the world. Common sense prevailed and she let him go without a word of protest.

CHAPTER SEVEN

"Want a bite?" Garth inquired lazily, offering Elisa first dibs on the apple he had been polishing on his shirt sleeve.

"Hmm . . . no thanks, I'm not hungry yet," she sighed, stretching her jean-clad legs out on the blanket beside his, arms pillowed behind her neck for support. "This is a lovely spot and it's so peaceful. However did you find it? Are you sure we aren't trespassing?" Even as she asked, Elisa knew she was too relaxed to care one way or the other.

"We are, but I know the owner. He won't mind," said the man, smiling and settling back against the trunk of the gnarled old tree that sprawled overhead, unmindful of the bits of bark that must have been digging into his back. The thin cotton shirt he wore could offer little protection. "God, it has been one hell of a week." The pastoral scene somehow took the sting out of his words. "How did yours go?"

"Well, it wasn't one of my best." She chose the words carefully, with only a fraction of the annoyance she had actually felt at the time. "I swear if one more person had asked me about our engagement, I would have gladly stuffed this ring down their throat. It seems that you and I are the seven-day wonder right now, especially after the announcement in the papers on Thursday."

Garth stirred, looking a little uncomfortable. "I tried to call you before that article was printed. The newspapers somehow got wind of our engagement so I had to make a statement. It seemed preferable to ending up as an item in the gossip columns. I'm sorry I couldn't let you know ahead of time. There wasn't any answer when I tried the apartment."

"That's all right. Believe me, it's a minor problem compared to writing Amanda and James," Elisa said with feeling. "I tried for three days and finally gave up. Oh, Garth, I didn't know what to say to them that would make any sense. This has all been so crazy."

"Look, Elisa, there's something I'd better tell you. I sent James and Amanda a telegram first thing Monday morning. An answer arrived just before I left my apartment today. Would you like me to read it to you?" He took a folded yellow paper from his shirt pocket.

She raised one eyebrow, but did not change her position. "Please do."

Garth proceeded to read it aloud. " 'Congratulations. Stop. You have our blessing. Stop. Charlotte and Reggie married Thursday and returning to England. Stop. Touring southern France while here. Stop. See you both in two weeks. Stop. All our love, Amanda and James. Stop.' " Garth refolded the telegram and returned it to his pocket.

"I suppose I should thank you," Elisa said in a tight voice, "though you do take a great deal upon yourself."

"I simply felt they deserved to know," Garth stated in a quiet voice, the expression he turned to her bearing no trace of apology. "It occurred to me that the cost of a transatlantic cable might be something you could ill afford."

"Perhaps you're right. Anyway, I'm glad they know. I

could imagine how hurt they would be if they found out through one of their friends or acquaintances. You know how fast good news travels." She sounded faintly dismayed.

"Oh, honey," he said, seeming to sense her dilemma.

"I—I don't mean to be ungrateful for what you've done," Elisa began to stammer an explanation. She swung her legs beneath her and sat up, reaching out to grasp one of his hands in hers. "It's—it's just that I'm not accustomed to having someone do things for me. It takes getting used to."

"I know."

"Anyway, it's too lovely a day to quarrel with anyone. Tell me, how was your week?" She released his hand and resumed her former position.

"Busy. Sometimes I feel like I spend more of my life talking about architecture and planning than I do creating. When that happens, I get in my car and come out here. Wright thought cities were evil incarnate. While I may not agree with him completely, I understand what he meant."

"You seem to know the area around Spring Green awfully well. I don't think I've ever been on so many back roads before in my life."

"Didn't I tell you?" He obviously thought he had. "I spent several years at Taliesin as a young man fresh out of college."

Elisa opened her eyes and looked at him in wonder. She had heard, of course, that Garth was a brilliant architect, but just how brilliant she was only now beginning to understand. "You studied with Frank Lloyd Wright?"

"No, Wright died in 1959, long before I was old enough to be an apprentice, but his philosophy is still perpetuated through the Taliesin Fellowship. Taliesin East, as it came to be called, is just over that next hill." Garth pointed off to the south. "The school is open for tours in the summer.

The house itself won't be open to the public while Mrs. Wright is still alive."

"Taliesin is such an unusual name."

"Actually, Taliesin was a Welsh poet. The name literally means 'shining brow.' Frank Lloyd Wright thought that description appropriate for the hillside he had chosen as the site for his home."

"Did you always want to be an architect?" Elisa inquired, deeply interested.

"No, not consciously anyway. I studied civil engineering at Wisconsin. Once I was graduated, I realized it wasn't what I wanted after all." Garth hesitated for a moment. "Are you sure you want to hear all of this?" A rich laugh followed his question.

"Oh, yes, I'd like to know everything about you," she blurted out, her color deepening despite her last-minute efforts to the contrary.

Garth leaned toward her in a suggestive manner. "That, too, can be arranged."

"So . . . you were graduated in engineering from the University of Wisconsin. Then what happened?" Elisa asked with forced calmness.

"I got lucky. I was one of a handful chosen to work and study at Taliesin. Ironically it wasn't until sometime later I found out that Wright had originally been an engineering student at Wisconsin himself. Madison did not have a school of architecture in his day. Still doesn't, for that matter. That was one reason he built Taliesin back in 1911. The Fellowship was started in 1932, and then six years later Taliesin West was built near Phoenix, Arizona."

"Have you been there, too?"

"Yes, we migrated back and forth between the two like a caravan of nomads. But it still amazes me, Elisa, the talent of that one man." Encouraged by her rapt attention, he went on. "It seems so simple today to say that 'form

133

follows function,' but if you look at what Wright designed out of stone and concrete over eighty years ago it shows what a visionary the man was. He believed that architecture should belong with its natural surroundings. Taliesin East was constructed of stone that came from right around here, while Taliesin West rises from the desert floor as if it had been a part of it from the beginning. Have you seen the Unitarian Church in Madison? He did that in 1950."

"It's very beautiful and very modern," Elisa heard herself say inadequately.

"Frank Lloyd Wright was designing 'modern' buildings and homes as early as 1893." Garth shook his head. "My one regret is that I never met the man."

Elisa was not unacquainted with men of genius, men who were preoccupied with their little corner of the world to the exclusion of all else. She had loved another man like that once—her father.

Oh, dear God! Elisa cried out to herself. What was she thinking she had loved *another* man like that? She didn't love Garth Brandau. She couldn't!

"Elisa . . ."

"Your work is very important to you, isn't it?" she said, chewing on her lip, not daring to look at the man beside her.

"I suppose when a man reaches my age and doesn't have a wife or family, he tends to get caught up in his professional life."

The young woman ventured to lift her head at last. "Or could it be that his profession is the reason a man like that doesn't have a wife or family?"

"Perhaps." Garth paused and then said in a different voice, "Say, I'm getting hungry. How about you?"

"I thought you'd never ask." Elisa managed to laugh. "I'm famished!"

"Let's see what we have in here," he said, lifting the lid

134

of the picnic hamper. "I must confess I didn't pack our lunch myself. Since I wasn't sure what you liked, I told the deli to put in some of everything. Hmm . . . corned beef on rye, rare roast beef on pumpernickel, date bread with cream cheese, crabmeat salad, relishes, cheeses, fruit, mints—ah, and a bottle of wine and two glasses. I don't believe they missed a thing."

"Missed anything? It's a feast!" Elisa eagerly dug in and helped him unpack the food.

"What would you like to begin with?" inquired Garth politely, playing the perfect host.

"Everything!" she exclaimed with the verve of a hungry child bursting in the door after school.

"I think I'll start with the same," he joined in, "just as soon as I uncork the wine."

It was some time later that Elisa stretched out in the afternoon sun, replete, content beyond words to simply be with this man, here and now.

"Would you like more wine?" came a sleepy sun-warmed voice in her ear.

"I couldn't eat or drink even one more drop. Hmm . . . it is nice here," she murmured rather inanely, ending with a yawn she took no pains to conceal.

As Elisa felt herself about to drift off, something stirred the wisps of hair around her face. She couldn't tell for certain whether it was a kiss or merely a gentle summer breeze.

She awakened to discover Garth's head cradled in her lap, her hands resting lightly on the broad shoulders within their reach. Elisa gazed down at the handsome features in repose, taking advantage of the opportunity to study the man as she had often wanted to, but had never dared while he was awake.

Garth Brandau was not a simple man to understand, but then it had been her experience that people rarely were simple. What complex creatures human beings were, she

135

sighed. Made up of all they have been, all they wished to be. Yet, here at least was a man worth knowing.

Then without warning it struck again, that funny, fuzzy sensation in the pit of her stomach. The need, almost painful in its intensity, to touch him, to run her hands down the lean male body and across the expanse of half-bare chest was more than Elisa could bear. She squeezed her eyes tightly shut and waited for the waves of desire that washed through her to subside. Was it only sexual desire that burned in her like a white-hot coal? Or was it the beginnings of something more? Something Elisa had been fighting to conceal even from herself.

She was suddenly afraid. It would not take much more for her to fall hopelessly, desperately, in love with this man, and that could only have disastrous results for her. She knew it as surely as she knew that theirs would never succeed as a platonic relationship. Still, love was often not the least bit wise. Elisa knew that as well.

With almost superhuman effort she eased Garth's head onto the blanket and got to her feet, needing at that moment to put some distance between herself and the sleeping male form. She stepped away from their place beneath the tree and stood on the crest of the hill, looking out at the small valley below. The first shadows of evening were gathering in the distant sky. They must have slept far longer than she had realized upon waking.

Elisa had no idea how long she stood there. It could have been five minutes or fifty, but they were some of the happiest in her life, if contentment equated with happiness. When her reverie was interrupted, as her sixth sense told her it would be, it was by soft footfalls in the grass behind her. It was followed by a deep masculine voice still struggling out of sleep.

"Whatever are you staring at so intently? You're scowling and it mars that pretty little face of yours," said Garth, slinging a casual arm about her shoulders, molding her to his side, where she fit like the missing piece of a jigsaw puzzle.

"Nothing really," she said. "I've been trying to decide if that's a house I see over there against the hillside, among those trees on the left, or my imagination working overtime again."

"It is a house."

"I can't imagine the mind capable of conceiving a place so perfectly suited to its surroundings. I wish I could see it up close," Elisa sighed, letting her head come to rest on the solid shoulder at her disposal.

"You can," stated Garth, as if he had no doubts she could.

"But how? I mean—" The girl stopped and gazed up at the man beside her. "It's—it's your house, isn't it?" She knew the answer even before he spoke.

"Yes, it is my house."

"This is part of your land." Elisa spread her hands as if to encompass the hill on which they stood and the valley below. "That's why you were so certain the owner wouldn't object to us being here."

"Would you really like to see the house?"

"Yes. Yes, I would," she said decidedly.

"Come on, then. We'll throw the picnic stuff in the trunk and drive over," Garth said easily.

"Okay." Elisa nodded, her manner calm, but inside she was aflutter with excitement and curiosity at the prospect of seeing his home.

The uniqueness of the structure was all the more awe-inspiring the nearer they came. It was nestled in a grove, low slung, composed of stone and native wood, almost Oriental in its simplicity of line. Yet it seemed as much a part of the Wisconsin countryside as the trees and rocks surrounding it.

Elisa had never seen a house quite like this one, but then she had never known a man like Garth before either.

There was a stark beauty, a passion, in its design that told her more of the man than any number of words possibly could. As a work of art personifies its creator, so did this house. That was when she knew. It was a strange way to discover she was in love with Garth, but love him she did.

He parked the sleek automobile in front of the house and came around to offer her his arm.

"Welcome to my home, Elisa," he said, unlocking the large double front door and bidding her enter.

"Oh, Garth—" Her voice cracked as she fought back a cry that seemed torn from lungs that could not breathe. Tears pricked her eyes, threatening to spill over onto her cheeks. "I—I had no idea—"

The room before them was dominated by a large fireplace forged from the same quarry that had yielded the stone for the outside. The wood, too, was repeated in the finely wrought furniture. To think that this man had created such beauty. It left Elisa shaken.

"I made most of the furniture in this room myself," he volunteered with just the right touch of modesty, rather unlike his usual manner. "It used to be a hobby of mine. I'm afraid I haven't had much time to indulge my hobbies lately."

The girl finally found her voice. "It is a shame."

"Yes, it is," Garth agreed, rubbing his mustache in a habitual gesture Elisa was beginning to recognize. "I've had a fine piece of wood waiting in my workshop for over a year now."

"No," she laughed lightly, "that's not what I meant."

"What did you mean, then?"

"Simply that it's a shame Frank Lloyd Wright never had the pleasure of meeting you." She turned away and ran her hand over the back of one of the chairs. It was smooth and cool to the touch like a shady spot by the river's edge. "Oh, I can see his influence here and there, but even he would never have built this house. Only you could have done that. It has your mark indelibly stamped on it. You are a romantic, Garth Brandau, whether you know it or not."

He took her gently by the shoulders and spun her around to face him. There was an expression in his green eyes Elisa had not seen there before. "I think I'll take that as a compliment."

"It was meant as one—truly," she uttered in a soft voice.

"You are going to make a very good psychologist, honey." Without further explanation he dropped a kiss on her upturned mouth. A mouth that wanted much more from him. "How about a glass of fresh-squeezed lemonade?"

The unexpected U-turn in their conversation caught her unaware. Consequently Elisa said the first thing that popped into her head. "Do you have a strainer?"

Garth looked at her as if she had lost her wits. "A strainer? What in the devil do you want with a strainer?" With hands on hips, he took a typically masculine stance and waited for her to answer.

"Well, I love lemonade, but I detest the little pieces of pulp," she said sheepishly. "It reminds me of the lumpy oatmeal my mother used to make me eat every morning for breakfast when I was a little girl. Ugh!" Elisa screwed up her nose in distaste.

Garth put his head back and let out a delighted whoop. "Come along, then, we'll see if we can find a strainer for your lemonade." He took her by the hand and pulled her along behind him into the kitchen.

"Be sure you have the right glass," the man instructed, sliding the patio door open. "I happen to prefer my lemonade with pulp."

"Yes, sir, Mr. Brandau," Elisa muttered under her breath.

"I thought we would sit out here," he said, indicating a table and chairs set up by the pool.

"Whew! It seems to have got warmer this evening," Elisa exclaimed between sips of her cold drink.

"How about a swim later?" asked Garth, casually stretching his long legs out in front of him.

"I'd love to."

"Did you bring a swimsuit with you?" Something flickered behind the man's eyes. "Not that it's absolutely necessary, of course."

The color sprinted into Elisa's face, just as they both guessed it would. "Yes, I have a suit with me, fortunately."

"That depends on your point of view, sweetheart." He gave a little grunt that might have been a laugh. "It is hot out here. Come on, I'll show you where you can change."

Garth escorted her to the bedroom next to his, leaving her at the doorway with a final admonishment. "If you need anything, just yell. I'll be right next door."

"I'll meet you poolside in ten minutes," Elisa carefully enunciated, closing the door in his grinning face.

Once inside she took a moment to study her surroundings, delighted by the room in which she found herself. The furnishings were sparse, but elegant. The double-size bed in the center of the room was covered by an azure spread of some marvelous material Elisa could not put a name to. It felt like silk, but refused to wrinkle. The same fabric had been creatively used on several walls in lieu of the more traditional wallpaper. It was a room decorated with a woman in mind. Elisa could only hope that woman was Garth's mother.

"Fat chance!" What started as a snicker soon grew into a genuine laugh. The idea *was* ridiculous.

Discovering she had daydreamed away nearly half of her ten minutes, Elisa quickly stripped off her clothes and slipped into the black bikini she took from her handbag.

140

It was a remarkable feat of engineering—two rather brief scraps of cloth that stayed on her body through a series of strategically placed bows. She knew she had a good figure, well-proportioned and rather long-legged for five foot five. She had worn this very bikini any number of times at the lake. It never failed to get an enthusiastic response. Why then the sudden desire for a beach jacket? she chided good-naturedly.

The young woman brushed her hair back from her face. With a well-executed twist and several bobby pins she secured it to the top of her head. A final check in the mirror and she was ready. With tummy tucked in and back straight, a towel she had found in the adjoining bathroom casually tossed over one shoulder, Elisa strolled out to the pool.

She was evidently the first one changed, for Garth was nowhere in sight. Dropping the towel by the pool's edge, she tested the water temperature with her big toe. It was cold to the uninitiated touch. Yet Elisa knew it would be the least painful method if she just jumped in all at once. To expose herself inch by inch was akin to slow torture.

"Oh, what the hell," she muttered, pulling the pins from her hair. With a shake of her brown mane she did a neat clean dive into the water.

"How very sensible of you, my dear." They were the first words Elisa heard upon surfacing.

"Garth Brandau—have you been watching me?" she sputtered, wiping the water from her face with one hand.

"Naturally. I can't think of anything I would rather do," he replied, smooth as a polished stone.

The man posed there by the side of the pool, laughing down at her, was a great temptation. Just one good splash . . . But Elisa restrained herself, knowing retribution would be swift if she dared. He was wearing a pair of brief swimmers' trunks that left little to the female imagination. Elisa supposed the same could be said of her own bikini.

Her eyes, curious and dark with desire, were riveted on the male figure. She studied it much as she would a piece of classical sculpture. Her gaze moved down the wide, well-shaped shoulders to the waistline, which she supposed remained unchanged since his college days, then along the muscular arms, whose strength she knew well enough for herself, to firm, straight hips. His bronzed skin seemed to invite her caress, a sprinkling of hair teased her with its masculinity. It was unfair somehow that one man should have it all.

"Oh, damn!" Elisa swore under her breath. Why did it have to be this man of all men?

"What did you say, honey?"

"Aren't you coming in?" she called up to him in an inviting manner.

"Yes," he answered, his eyes never leaving hers. "I'll just switch on the underwater lights." A moment later the pool lit up. Then with an expertly done dive Garth joined her.

She saluted him with a brief nod. "You do that rather well, Mr. Brandau."

"As do you, Miss Harrington."

"Do you manage to do everything equally well?" She arched a brow in his direction.

"I think you should judge that for yourself," he replied with what looked suspiciously like a broad grin.

"I'll race you two lengths of the pool." The challenge was issued without mention that Elisa had been a member of both her high school and college swim teams.

"You're on!" Garth assented quickly.

The girl was immediately wary. He was too eager, had agreed too fast. It did not take long to find out why. Even with a head start she had not requested, Garth beat her by half a length.

"Congratulations . . . you're very good," she conceded, slightly winded and more than a little nonplussed.

"So are you." He paused in his triumph. "I have to confess, you didn't have a chance. I swim twenty laps every morning at the club pool."

"You might have told me," she sniffed over one shoulder, swimming for the edge. In one fluid movement Elisa pulled herself from the water and picked up her towel. Putting her head down, she began to rub the long tendrils of wet hair.

"Where did you learn to swim like that?" He had followed her out of the pool.

"Swim team."

"High school?"

"Yes, and college."

"You might have mentioned that."

"Good heavens, no, man, I was trying to hustle you. Brrrr!" Elisa shivered. "I guess I better go in and get dressed. I'm freezing all of a sudden."

"I have a better idea." Garth took her by the hand and led her a few feet away to a small circular pool that had gone unnoticed by Elisa.

"A few minutes in the Jacuzzi are all you need, honey. It'll have you warmed up in no time. Just step down and make yourself comfortable on that tiled bench. I want to get us a glass of wine."

It was the next best thing to heaven, just as Garth had said it would be, all warmth and relaxation with its gentle churning motion sending the water swirling about her legs. When the man reappeared a few minutes later with two glasses of pale white wine, the last vestiges of cold had seeped from Elisa's fingers and toes.

"Hmm, thank you." She lazily accepted the glass offered to her. "This is very good."

"German . . . Moselblümchen," he replied, slipping into the Jacuzzi.

They sipped their wine in silence, seemingly of mutual

accord, savoring the uninterrupted peace and quiet of the summer night.

Elisa set her glass on the edge of the pool and spread her arms out on either side of her, freeing her legs to float in front of her body. She did not realize the action strained the top of her bikini against her breasts, clearly outlining them down to the smallest detail.

"Feeling better now?" Garth inquired, sliding along the bench until their thighs met.

"Y-yes, thank you." Her breathing seemed constricted.

His hand found Elisa's bare midriff beneath the water's surface. It caressed her in slow sensuous movements that set her all aquiver. His other hand came up to rest on her shoulder.

Garth's breath wafted hot and sweet against her skin. "I'm glad we had today by ourselves, honey."

"So am I." The young woman was very much afraid her voice came out as a squeak. The nearness of the man was causing her heart to perform odd little rhythms against her ribs. Elisa had the strangest premonition the entire day had been building up to this one moment.

He sucked in a breath as if it were his last. "Lord, Elisa, but you're lovely." Instead of drawing her closer as she expected, he thrust her away from him.

"You can laugh"—of course, she did nothing of the kind—"but I couldn't get you out of my mind all week." His own laughter emerged harsh and self-deprecating. "The days were rough enough. You should have seen me in that meeting in Milwaukee on Thursday. They had to repeat everything twice. I know most of them thought I was hung over. Maybe I was."

"Garth—" she said with a sort of groan.

"Wait, there's more, sweetheart. The nights were worse. I couldn't get any sleep unless I worked myself into oblivion first. The first night or two I honestly thought it was because I've been driving myself hard at my work. It

144

didn't take long to figure out that was only half the problem. A sad state of affairs for a man of thirty-five, wouldn't you say?" He impatiently threaded his fingers through still-wet hair that was starting to wave around his ears.

"I thought I'd been through it all, but I was wrong. I can't take much more of this, Elisa. I want you so badly, it's like a gnawing hunger that won't be satisfied, eating away at my insides. Hell, I don't know why I'm telling you any of this." The man let loose with a string of profanity.

"Now look, Garth . . ." She obviously found his confession a little hard to swallow.

"Ah, I see you don't believe me." He crooked a faintly sardonic brow in her direction. "But then maybe you don't know what it is to really want someone," he hissed, his anger rising between them like a tangible force.

"Are you crazy or something? You silly man, I'm half in love—" Elisa clamped a hand over her mouth, but too late . . . too late! "Garth Brandau, if you made all of this up just to lead me on, so help me God, I'll—I'll—"

"I swear it's all true," he laughed lightly, triumphantly. The sound made her uneasy. All of a sudden she wasn't so sure what the truth was.

"Don't think about things so much, darling," Garth murmured against her mouth. "Isn't it enough to know that I want you until it rips my guts apart? Come here, Elisa, I need you to put me out of my misery."

Elisa had no chance to respond with any words of her own. Not that she thought to. Garth bent forward, his mouth coming down on hers with a bruising force. He was determined to show her he spoke the truth, that he did indeed desire her until it hurt, nearly hurting her in the process.

As he moved eagerly against her she could feel the steel wall of his chest with its prickly spray of hair rub along her bare skin. She could have sworn the temperature in the

Jacuzzi shot up ten degrees as their heated bodies met in a fierce embrace.

He knew all the moves, this man, gently kneading the small of her back until she was forced to arch toward him, all too aware that their lack of clothing made it seem they were locked in a lovers' embrace with nothing to keep them apart. Elisa was conscious of every delicious bone and muscle and the ultimate proof of his need for her as Garth pulled her alongside him.

She almost hated him for the suspicions lurking in the back of her mind. Had it been no more than a line he was handing her? Elisa intoned a silent prayer that it wasn't so. Then she felt herself drowning in the man's kiss. His breath became hers, his hands performing miracles as they moved over her body, the flimsy bikini no obstacle to his explorations.

Once she was all soft and pliant, Garth's mouth began to play games with her. First teasing, then cajoling, then demanding, until her senses were swirling with him.

Elisa's own hands stirred from the thick thatch of hair at the back of his neck, where they had somehow become entangled, and meandered across the expanse of broad shoulders and lower to the taut abdomen.

With a single fingernail she traced the outline of his navel, rewarded to feel Garth shudder at her touch. Throwing her inhibitions aside, Elisa ran her hands along the inside of his waistband, wondering for a moment what he must look like without the trunks he was wearing. The vision would have taken her breath away, if she had been able to breathe, that is.

"Dear God!" she whispered against his neck, her lips suddenly parched.

His answer was a low animallike moan. He pulled her onto his lap, reminiscent of another night and another place. He laid her back in his arms as though she were the feast and he the dinner guest. His tongue and lips wreaked havoc with her nervous system as he licked the tiny drops of water from her skin. Finding the tip of her breast through the material of her bikini, he nipped at the peak until it bloomed in invitation. In two swift movements the ties of her top were undone and her breasts floated free. She turned her head just as the top was swished away in the churning water.

"You drive me out of my mind, Elisa!"

Could the husky, strangled whisper scarcely audible to her ears have come from Garth? There was little time to ponder the possibility as his tongue rolled around first one nipple and then the other, savoring the taste and touch of her. If that was not enough for the man, his mouth lay siege to one pink mound while his hand serviced the second.

Elisa's heart was throbbing like a jungle drum when he finally relented. Garth's features were darkly flushed, his breathing labored.

"If we keep this up, we'll both no doubt drown here and now and not even care," he laughed raggedly. "But what a way to go!"

The man stood up and stepped from the Jacuzzi with Elisa still in his arms. He plucked a velour towel from a lawn chair as he walked by, and wrapped it around her. She seemed to weigh no more than a small child as Garth carried her across the patio and through the sliding glass door that led to his bedroom.

Once they were inside, he helped Elisa regain a steady stance, setting her on her own two feet. He gently took the towel from her hands and proceeded to give her a rub-down, first attacking the tangle of damp curls that careened over one shoulder, then down the milky-white throat, and lastly in a leisurely fashion around each bare breast.

Garth's fingers next sought and found the curve of her hips. A casual flick of his wrist and the panties of her bikini were dispensed with. They dropped soundlessly to the thick lush carpet. When he knelt to caressingly run the towel between her thighs and down each slender leg, a hot tide rose up inside Elisa that she could do nothing to extinguish. Her head was forced back with a whimper of surrender.

When she knew she could take no more, Garth straightened up and offered her the towel. She took it from him and held it in front of her, staring at it, realizing he wanted her to imitate his actions. When she dared to look up, it was to find him as God had created the species, his trunks having joined her bikini on the floor.

In a tentative gesture Elisa reached out and began to dry the mat of hair on his chest, her hands all aquiver. She stroked each arm in turn before turning her attention to the narrow hips, her body working hard to keep the air going in and out of her lungs. She was aware of this man in a way she had never been aware before.

The towel was tossed to one side as the man caught her face between hardened palms, compelling her to meet his gaze.

"I want to make love to you, Elisa. You know that, don't you?" Garth waited for her to acknowledge his question and the full implication behind it.

She exhaled tremulously. "Yes."

He caught hold of her by the shoulders, gripping her so tightly, she winced. "Oh, honey, don't look at me like that. If you don't stop me now, there isn't a chance in hell we won't end up in that bed together."

She held his eyes unswervingly, somehow unmindful of the pain caused by his hands. The next thing Elisa knew her feet left the ground and Garth was pressing her down into the bed.

"So sweet . . ." he murmured, "so very sweet." His tongue drew a path around one small ear, then along the

well-defined bones of her jaw, until he found her mouth
in a kiss that exploded with desire, with insatiable hunger.

Elisa felt her need rise up to meet his. A wild bird's cry
that mounted to the sky in response. She gloried in the
mastery of his touch as Garth lowered himself to her with
an urgency that was still gentleness itself. Caught up in the
eye of a hurricane as she was, everything swirled around
her with incredible force.

His kisses soon became a necessity, his touch an addic-
tion, as Elisa arched her body to meet his, wanting this as
she had never wanted anything before in her life.

When the jarring ring of the telephone penetrated the
sensual haze surrounding them, they both reacted in turn.

"Oh, no . . ." Elisa cried, burying her face in the pillow.
Not now! she wanted to scream.

Garth's reaction was immediate and violent. A word of
profanity pierced the air as he rolled away from Elisa and
grabbed the offending instrument from the bedside table.
With a terrible yank on the cord he intended to fling the
telephone across the room. Instead he simply knocked the
receiver from the hook as the telephone bounced off a
nearby chair and landed at the man's feet. They could
both hear a distressed female voice call out, muffled
though it was by the carpet.

"Garth? Garth, it's Mother. Are you all right?"

He stood up and bent over to retrieve the telephone,
making no attempt to cover himself as he did.

"Hello, Mother. No, everything is fine. I accidentally
knocked the phone off the table, that's all." Garth turned
around and gave the still supine Elisa a broad wink. "No,
Mother, you didn't interrupt anything important. I've
been working hard and thought I would relax here at
home tonight." He sat down on the edge of the bed and
reached for a cigarette from a box on the night table.

The young woman lay there trying to comprehend that
while she was still trembling from the inside out with

sexual anticipation, he had apparently recovered and was settling down for an amiable chat with his mother.

Elisa cringed on the bed beside Garth. The bastard—to bring her to the point of capitulation only to leave her high and dry! She slid off the mattress, taking no cares not to disturb the man on the other side. With quaking hands she picked up the discarded bikini and towel from the bedroom floor and wrapped the latter about her nude form. She had almost got to the door when Garth called out to her.

"Elisa!" came the hoarse whisper. "Please, don't go!" He looked horribly annoyed.

She dealt him a glacial stare. "And why not? After all, nothing *important* was interrupted, was it?" With as much aplomb as she could muster under the circumstances, she made her exit.

Once in the hallway she began to tremble all over. Was it the night breeze brushing against her bare skin or a delayed reaction to the fact she had just nearly made love with a man who did not love her? Elisa did not want to think about that right now. There would be plenty of time for self-recriminations later.

She ran for the bedroom allocated for her use. Throwing the towel down, she pulled on her clothes. Her anger gradually dissipated as she reminded herself it was no more Garth's fault they had been interrupted than it was hers. It wasn't anyone's fault. Sometimes these things simply happened.

Regaining some semblance of composure, Elisa acknowledged she should perhaps be grateful for that fateful telephone call from Garth's mother. It had saved her from making possibly the biggest mistake of her twenty-five years. It might have been a story with a different ending if theirs were a genuine romance . . . if Garth truly loved her. But he didn't. To continue would have only put her

150

in a position of heartbreaking vulnerability, loving him as she did.

Elisa was vigorously toweling her hair when she heard the bedroom door open behind her. She did an abrupt about-face as Garth came barging into the room with little regard for propriety. Not that their relationship wasn't long past propriety, Elisa grimly reminded herself.

"Didn't your mother ever teach you to knock?" she asked testily, noting he had slipped into a pair of jeans if not a shirt before seeking her out. To her chagrin, she found her eyes straying to the smattering of hair that sinuated down his chest to the point where it disappeared beneath the waistband of his pants.

"I'm in no mood to play verbal games with you, Elisa," Garth ground through his teeth. "No one is sorrier than I am that we were interrupted when we were, believe me. Damn!" The man wrapped his arms around her. "I am sorry, honey. I could hardly hang up on my own mother though."

"I know." Elisa's voice came out soft and small, ill-concealing her disappointment. Yet there was an element of relief in it, as well.

Garth affectionately kissed her cheek. "By the way, my mother is flying in tomorrow and would like to meet the two of us for lunch on Monday. Do you think you'd be able to make it?"

"I suppose so," she answered absently, at the moment more concerned with the incessant pounding going on inside her head than anything. The pain seemed to have come from nowhere. "I—I've got a rotten headache, Garth. It must have been the wine. Would you mind taking me home now?"

Obviously he did mind. A knowing look of defeat darted across the man's face, but he merely gave her a brisk nod. "If you say so, Elisa."

151

"I'll be glad when the whole stupid thing is over!" She choked down a sob, gathering up her belongings.

"Believe me, you won't be the only one applauding when this damn charade has run its course!"

The man's words were words of frustration and impatience—even anger—but the light in his smoldering eyes carried another message if Elisa had only thought to glance his way. She wearily slung the beach bag over one arm and walked out of the bedroom, not bothering to even look back.

CHAPTER EIGHT

Elisa smoothed down the skirt of her white summer suit, took a deep steadying breath, and entered the hotel restaurant. She looked around expectantly as the maître d' came forward to greet her.

"Yes, miss," said the man with a slight nod of the head.

"I'm meeting Mr. Brandau . . . Mr. Garth Brandau. Would you please show me to his table?"

"Of course, Miss—ah . . ."

She quelled the urge to giggle and put on her best social demeanor. "Miss Harrington."

"Please follow me, miss. Mr. Brandau's table is this way." He led her to a choice location where a table was appropriately set for three. "Neither of the other parties has arrived yet, Miss Harrington, but I will have the waiter take your order if you would care for a drink."

"Thank you," she responded, graciously accepting his offer of a chair.

Elisa sat sipping a glass of Chablis, gazing about the tastefully decorated room, occasionally glancing toward the entranceway then down at her watch, one foot unconsciously tapping the floor beneath the table. It was ten minutes past the appointed hour, yet there was still no sign of Garth or his mother.

Just then a middle-aged woman entered the restaurant. After a brief, but friendly, exchange with the maître d', she turned in Elisa's direction, a surprisingly warm smile on her round, ageless face.

Could this maternal creature with the salt-and-pepper hair and a figure bordering on the stout possibly be Garth's mother? For some reason Elisa had envisioned her as the sleek Fifth Avenue type, designer-dressed and imposing in an "old money" sort of way. Instead here was a rather ordinary woman, well-groomed certainly, but hardly Bonwit Teller.

The young woman rose to her feet as a cordial hand was extended.

"Hello, my dear, I'm Helen McCormack and you must be Miss Harrington."

"Elisa, please. How nice to meet you, Mrs. . . . . McCormack." The hesitation in her voice gave her away.

"Oh, dear, I see that my son has been remiss. You were expecting me to introduce myself as Helen Brandau, weren't you?" She inquired, kindness itself in her tone.

"Yes, I suppose I was," Elisa murmured sheepishly. She blushed right down to her roots, all the while cursing Garth for not telling her at least that much and herself for getting into this mess in the first place.

"Hasn't Garth told you anything about his family?" Helen gently prodded after placing her own order for a glass of wine.

"Very little, I'm afraid. Ours has been a rather whirl-wind relationship. I do know that Mr. Brandau is or was an attorney and that Garth did not wish to follow in his footsteps. Professionally, that is." Elisa stumbled over her thoughts. "But please, Mrs. McCormack, no one owes me any explanations."

The woman gave Elisa's hand one of those maternal

pats. "Don't distress yourself, my dear, and I would like it if you could call me Helen." Her smile was sympathetic and understanding. The girl felt herself instantly warming to her. "You had no way of knowing that Garth's father and I were divorced many years ago. I'm married to a wonderful man named Paul McCormack and have been for nearly twenty years. I see *that* does surprise you," the woman shrewdly observed.

Elisa suddenly realized there were a great many things she did not know about the man she was supposedly engaged to, things a real fiancée would doubtless be aware of, she told herself.

"Don't judge Garth too harshly. His family was once a very painful subject for him, perhaps it still is. We never had that closeness that some families are lucky enough to have. Ah, here's my drink. Whatever is this?" Helen McCormack accepted a folded note from the waiter. She scanned the brief message and handed it over to Elisa without a word.

"Garth won't be joining us for lunch," the younger woman repeated aloud as it finally sunk in.

"Like father, like son, I'm afraid." This time Helen's statement was punctuated with a deep sigh. "Perhaps it's just as well. This will give the two of us a chance to talk. Shall we order now?"

"Yes, of course." Elisa shook free of the inertia that had struck her upon reading Garth's message. A business emergency, her foot! The least she could do under the circumstances was pass a pleasant hour over lunch with this very nice woman who believed Elisa to be engaged to her son.

During a sumptuous meal of cold lobster and salad, their talk flowed as freely as the wine. Elisa was surprised by how much Garth had evidently told his mother about her.

"My son tells me you had an unusually close relationship with your father. I think he was a little envious. It was not that way between him and his father. But then I don't need to tell you about the consequences. I'm sure you see them for yourself and probably understand better than most people. I know you're a graduate student in psychology." Helen sought confirmation of her facts. "Have you made up your mind what you would like to do with it?"

"Yes, eventually I want to get my Ph.D. in the area of clinical psychology. I must confess that's beyond my pocketbook at the moment. Meanwhile I plan to work at a local clinic and save my money. I've been spending one day a week there now as part of the work on my master's degree." Elisa looked up to see the other woman staring off into the distance. "I'm afraid I've been boring you. I didn't mean to go on so," Elisa laughed, after making a rather detailed account of why she wanted to work with family counseling.

"Not in the least, my dear." Helen McCormack brought her attention back to her companion. "I was thinking how different things are for a young woman today than they were when I was your age. If only I had known then what I do now." Her laugh was light and a little sad. "But I have never been one for regrets and I won't start now." She ran a finger around the rim of her wineglass. "I want my son to be happy, Elisa. What mother doesn't? Are you very much in love with him?" Clear green eyes, so much like Garth's, were raised to the girl's. No idle curiosity there, only the genuine concern of a mother for her only child.

Elisa gave an answer that came straight from her heart. "Yes, I am. I can't pretend to explain how it happened." She threw up her hands with a self-conscious laugh. "I've asked myself that question again and again the past few weeks. I am normally not an impulsive person, you see. Garth is obviously an attractive man. When it comes to

156

his profession, I know he is considered a rare talent, but I knew that I loved him when I saw the house out by Spring Green."

"Definitely his finest work," concurred Helen. "He put his soul into that place. I'm glad you saw that."

"I once told someone that you could tell it was the real thing if it was like finding the other half of yourself. I still believe that, but love isn't that simple."

Helen vigorously nodded her head in agreement. "It never is that simple. I suppose because for a woman love is everything, for a man it's a thing apart. That isn't an exact quote, by the way, nor do I seem to recall who said it, nonetheless it is often true."

Elisa was familiar with the quote. It was "Man's love is of man's life a thing apart, 'Tis woman's whole existence," and Lord Byron had said it, yet none of this did she say aloud.

With her usually gentle brow marred by a thoughtful frown, she began to speak. "I can't agree with that sentiment myself. I would not allow a man or a child or anyone to be the only thing in my life. A man may be the most important thing to me, but he would never be my whole world. I don't believe it would be fair to either of us if I did that." Elisa's strong, clear voice showed how sincerely she felt. "What an awful responsibility to put on another human being. To say to someone you love, 'You are everything to me, what you do makes me happy or unhappy.' There is only one person who can do that for us—and that's ourselves." Then she laughed right out loud. "Oh, dear, I've been lecturing again, haven't I?"

"Yes, but I don't mind in the least. You are so young and yet so wise. I'm rather envious actually. If I had realized at your age how different it all might have been for me, it could have prevented a lot of heartache for a lot of people." Helen took a sip of wine and leaned toward her dining companion. "Elisa, I want to tell you about Garth's

157

father and me. It just might help you to understand my son a little better."

It was then that Elisa nearly blurted out the truth about her relationship with Garth. It wasn't right somehow that she should be privy to this woman's secrets under false pretenses. She wanted desperately to be honest with Helen. It would be a relief, too, to tell someone the real story. Yes, but while it might make her feel better, what about Helen McCormack's feelings? Elisa knew the answer to that.

"I would like to know more about Garth's family life. I admit to some curiosity about it."

"I scarcely know where to begin," the older woman confessed with a self-conscious laugh. "I suppose at the beginning is the logical place." She took a deep breath and plunged ahead.

"I was twenty when I married Joseph Brandau, Madison's most eligible bachelor. It was the match of the season, as one social columnist put it. I was fresh out of an eastern finishing school and Joseph was already a successful attorney, ten years my senior. I was young and idealistic and so very much in love. Joseph was one of those curious men who had got along quite well without a wife. He saw no earthly reason why there should be any changes made just because he now had one. There was a pattern, an order, to his life. I was the natural one to adjust. After all, wasn't that a wife's duty?

"At first I honestly thought I could change him. What woman doesn't think she can change her man?" There was a wry little smile on Helen's face.

"People are capable of change," Elisa interposed.

"Perhaps so, but you will grant it's more difficult for some than others. Oh, don't get me wrong, Elisa, my story was no different than that of thousands of women. I married a man who was already set in his ways, who was wrapped up in his work to the virtual exclusion of every-

158

thing else. It was always one emergency after another, one more important trial, one more case that kept him late at the office." The woman paused, as if to catch her breath before going on.

"I was very lonely and I hadn't expected to feel lonely after I was married. I was one of those who were unprepared for the realities of adulthood. Still, Joseph and I might have made it work if he had met me halfway," she said without rancor.

"But he didn't?" Elisa murmured, enthralled with the story.

"He couldn't. He didn't know how. I finally realized it had to do with the way our culture defines men, the way men define themselves. We don't introduce a man by saying here is a thoughtful husband or a wonderful father or a good friend. No, it was always Joseph Brandau, attorney-at-law. Well, he was that first, foremost, and always."

The conversation lapsed long enough for the two of them to order coffee and dessert.

"When we were expecting our first child, I told myself that Joseph might mellow with fatherhood. He was in court brilliantly defending a hit-and-run driver the day Garth was born. When I miscarried with our second child, he was at an A.B.A. meeting in New York. I was alone when the doctor explained why I couldn't have any more children." She left an eloquent pause. "It was then I knew nothing would ever change Joseph Brandau."

Elisa reached for the woman's hand and held it in her own. "You must not go on if this is painful for you, Helen. I wouldn't want to cause you any more hurt."

"You are a sweet thing, but I came to grips with it a long time ago. I had to to survive. All I feel now is a kind of sadness for that young woman I once was. The saddest part is that what happened to me wasn't unique."

"If you're sure . . ." Elisa admitted to herself that she wanted to hear the end of the tale.

"Well, for a few years I did what many women did in those days, and still do: I filled my life trying to be the perfect mother. There was little I could do to change the father, but the son was a different matter." The crooked smile on her face revealed her uncertainty about whether she had succeeded or not.

"When Garth went off to school, I devoted my time to worthwhile charitable organizations, ladies clubs, church activities. The day came, of course, when that wasn't enough. My son was growing up. He needed me less and less—or so it seemed. I decided to take charge of my own future and signed up for a few classes at the university. There I was, a thirty-six-year-old college freshman!"

"Good for you, Helen!" A spontaneous cheer came from Elisa.

"W-why, thank you." The woman went flush with pleasure. "I thought the psychologist in you might approve. I recall Joseph Brandau patted me on the head as if to say 'Girls will be girls' when I told him. It was promptly dismissed from his mind as unimportant. You see, it was all some 'bee' the wife had in her 'bonnet' to him." Helen McCormack's eyes were shining now. "I loved my classes, especially those in anthropology. I had a secret dream to pursue it as a career someday. Then in my second year of studies I found myself in love with one of my professors . . . and he with me.

"Paul McCormack was five years my junior. He was everything Joseph was not. He believed in the dignity of the individual, the importance of every human being. They weren't just pretty words to Paul, he really lived them. For the first time in my life I was taken seriously. I don't need to tell you how wonderful that was after being married to a man like Joseph for seventeen years. Poor Joseph . . . he never did understand."

Elisa was following her words with the closest attention. "What did you do then?"

160

"I went along for another year, keeping Paul at arm's length, until the day of reckoning came and I knew I had to make a decision. It was the turning point in my life. It was now or never for me. My parents were horrified, Joseph was sure I had lost my mind, and my son was puzzled and hurt. Don't judge me too harshly, Elisa, but I chose Paul, knowing full well under the circumstances I would never be given custody of my son."

"It's not my place to judge what you did, Helen. And Garth was no longer a child, surely he understood."

"He was nearly fifteen and although the divorce was handled discreetly, he was bitter for a time. Later on, Garth made an effort to see me more often and to get to know Paul. By then we were married and living in Princeton, New Jersey."

"And Mr. Brandau—what happened to him?"

"Joseph died of a heart attack when Garth was twenty. He was fifty-three at the time."

Elisa found her curiosity had got her into rather an awkward situation. "I am sorry."

"I was saddened when I heard, naturally, but it was all a long time ago, and I was and am happily married to another man." Helen McCormack's face relaxed into a smile.

"He's a very lucky man too," Elisa added for good measure.

"We both feel lucky to have a partnership in marriage and in our professional lives. I'm Paul's assistant and we have been to the most fascinating spots of the world on our digs. We're headed for California next month to work on a project that could well prove that the cradle of man is right here in the United States. We'll be using a new method of dating that may well show the American Indian to be the forerunners of the European and Asian peoples. Oh, dear, now who's the one lecturing?" laughed Helen.

"No, it's fascinating." Elisa's protest was sincere.

"Well, I wish we had more time to talk, but I've promised to meet some old friends in less than a half hour. I've enjoyed our lunch together more than you know, Elisa. I'm going to like having you for a daughter-in-law. My son is a lucky man. I hope he realizes that."

The young woman placed a resounding kiss on Helen McCormack's cheek. "I'm very glad I had this chance to meet you. I think Garth is lucky to have you for his mother."

The two women exchanged a few words of good-bye and assurances that they would meet again soon. Then it was out into the afternoon sun, where they went their separate ways.

The luncheon date with Helen McCormack had taken place on Monday. It was now Wednesday and Elisa Harrington was preparing to make an early night of it. Shadowy smudges beneath her eyes attested to the fact that she had not been sleeping particularly well. With tight-lipped resolve she drew back the covers and crawled between the fresh sheets—sheets she had put on her bed that afternoon during a flurry of therapeutic housecleaning.

Nearly an hour later audible sighs could still be heard coming from the darkened room. The bedside lamp went on and a wide-eyed Elisa swung her long legs over the edge of the bed and sat up. Perhaps a cup of hot tea would do the trick.

It had been like this since returning to the apartment on Monday afternoon. She had tried to study, but with one ear listening for the telephone, anticipating its ring, and her expecting to answer and hear Garth's voice on the other end apologizing for his desertion at a crucial time, little had been accomplished by the girl.

The call never came. Finally, out of sheer frustration, Elisa put her books aside and joined in a fervor of fudge-making with her roommate. Between the two of them, they managed to consume the entire batch of candy at a single sitting, decrying men and their exasperating ways. They further indulged themselves by watching a three-hankie movie on the late show, unmindful that the small black and white set flickered with mathematical precision.

By this evening, with still not a word from Garth, Elisa's temperature had risen several points on the Celsius scale. During the past sixty-odd hours her emotions had run the gamut. She had been puzzled and frustrated at first, then simply hurt by his apparent lack of thoughtfulness, and finally angry. Phony engagement or no phony engagement, he had no right to treat her this way! Who did Garth Brandau think he was anyway?

She had not forgiven him for his failure to show up for their luncheon date with Helen McCormack, not by a long shot. Even more for not giving her some warning, some inkling of the circumstances surrounding his family. Then not to contact her for three whole days. To put it politely, she was royally steamed.

Perhaps, Elisa thought to herself as she put the tea kettle on to boil, just perhaps she could see the man now without spitting in his eye. But Garth had one hell of a lot of explaining to do in her book.

The young woman had her cup of tea and fifteen minutes later was sleepily crawling back into bed. Her last conscious thought was of the man who had occupied them the past few days nearly to the exclusion of all else. She was fifty kinds of fool to have fallen in love with him, she told herself . . . but it was with Garth's name on her lips that she drifted off into dreams.

Fighting her way out of a deep sleep, Elisa groped for the clock on the bedside table, knocking it off onto the floor. It took her a minute or two to realize it wasn't her alarm ringing after all, but the doorbell. She groggily wondered if Brenda had gone out without her key to the apartment. Her roommate was working a special banquet at the hotel tonight and had been running late when Elisa had last seen her. It seemed she had forgotten her key in the rush.

She slipped on a lightweight summer robe and made her way to the door, voicing the other girl's name as she jerked it open.

"Brenda—"

It was not Brenda.

"Just what in the hell do you think you're doing?" demanded an angry male voice.

"I presumed I was answering the doorbell," she said blithely, disregarding the dark, disapproving scowl on Garth's face and the strange clammerings of her heart at the sight of him.

"You have no business opening this door until you know who is on the other side," he started to lecture. "Use your head, woman. It could have been anyone."

"Well, it wasn't," she came back, not bothering to mask her annoyance. "Now if that's all you have to say to me, it *is* late and I *was* asleep."

"I'm sorry I woke you up, but I thought—evidently mistakenly so—that you might be glad to see me. I've been tied up in meetings every minute of the past three days. This was the first chance I've had to break away," Garth explained in a cool tone, the expression he turned to her bearing no trace of apology.

"You don't owe me any explanations as to your where-abouts." Elisa knew she was being deliberately contrary, but she didn't care somehow. By God, if she wanted to be mad, then she would be! "After all, it isn't as if we were really engaged," she added for good measure.

"That's true," Garth conceded with a casual air that matched her own.

The fact that he so readily agreed with her proved to be unexpectedly hurtful. It was like a knife being twisted in her midsection.

164

"I wanted to drop by to thank you for being so nice to my mother when I couldn't make it to our lunch date on Monday."

The young woman made a disparaging sound. "You don't have to thank me. It's very easy to be nice to Helen. She's a very nice woman."

"All right, so we've established that my mother is a nice woman." Garth's patience was wearing thin. "For God's sakes, Elisa, do we have to hold this conversation out here in the hallway? The least you could do is ask me in for a few minutes."

"Suit yourself," Elisa said waspishly, stepping aside to grant him entry.

Garth eased himself down on the sofa as if it somehow pained him. One hand went to his necktie to loosen the knot as he put his head back.

"God, I could use a cup of coffee," Garth exhaled wearily.

"I think this is where I came in," muttered Elisa. A reference to that first night when she had come in from work to find Garth waiting for her. That had been less than two weeks ago. How had this man managed to turn her world topsy-turvy in a mere ten days? Why had she allowed it? In her heart Elisa knew the answer to the second question, if not the first.

Garth lifted his head and stared at her with something akin to exhaustion in his green lightless eyes.

"What did you say?"

She did not have the heart to repeat her remark. He did look beat, and though she promised herself she would not forget her anger, she heard herself agreeing to make him some coffee.

"Forget the coffee, at least for now. Come here, honey." His voice had taken on that caressing quality she knew all too well. It immediately put Elisa on her guard. He wasn't going to charm his way out of this one. Nevertheless her body moved toward him as if it had a mind of its own, stopping only a few inches from the sofa.

"Yes?" she posed with a watery smile.

"I've needed to do this for three days," said Garth, reaching out a lazy hand.

The next thing Elisa knew she was enthroned on Garth's lap. His hands were burning her flesh through the flimsy material of her robe. A surprisingly soft mouth was asking her not to be angry with him but to give of her solace and understanding at a time when he needed both. Despite her better intentions, the girl found herself giving him all that he asked and more.

"These past few days have been hellish," he mumbled as his lips trailed across her throat to find the tender lobe of an ear. "You feel so damn good!"

The words exploded against her mouth as he recaptured it with his own. This time it could scarcely be called a kiss. Garth's mouth was making love to her with a fierce, passionate hunger. He overwhelmed Elisa, swallowing up her very soul with his intensity.

"Come to bed with me, Elisa. It's what we both want, and I need you the way a man needs a woman." His words were all satin and velvet, his voice deepened by the sexual desire he could not nor did not try to hide from her.

It took a few moments for his words to register through the sensual cocoon that had been spun around her. Yes, Garth needed her, wanted her in the physical sense, but where were the whispered words of love she could have told him would have assured him success? Why was the one word always missing from his vocabulary—"love"?

Because he didn't love her and she had been a stupid little ninny to ever have imagined that he might! Theirs was a relationship built solely on sexual attraction, temporary at best, and she was a "permanent" sort of girl. She was also supposed to be madder than hops at the man. He hadn't bothered to call her for three whole days, and yet the minute he showed up on her doorstep, she had practically fallen into his arms. There weren't enough ways to call her a fool!

With this stern lecture delivered to herself, Elisa surreptitiously wiped away the one tear that had managed to escape, and pulled back from Garth's embrace.

"Now what's wrong?" he asked, unhooding his eyelids.

Elisa felt resentment rise up inside her like a tidal wave. She had to remind herself to breathe. "I'll tell you what's wrong. *You're* what's wrong, Garth Brandau!" She was shaking from head to toe, only partially because of his lovemaking; it was mostly due to plain old-fashioned anger.

"Ah, c'mon, honey. I'm too tired to play guessing games with you." He clasped her hips between his hands and pulled her to him. "We have a lot of time to make up for." She saw the familiar light of desire go on in his eyes.

"Let go of me, Garth." Elisa, made all the angrier by hearing her voice shake, shook off his hands. "I told you before I will not have a casual affair with you. I meant it then and I mean it now."

"Believe me, any affair between the two of us would never be casual, sweetheart." He twisted the last word so that it came out with wry humor. "After all, we are engaged." Garth said it as if that should somehow make a difference.

"You know as well as I do that it's not a real engagement," she muttered through numb lips.

"But it could be . . ." Garth said in a quiet voice. He passed a weary hand across his eyes. "Hell, I'm not putting this very well." He seemed to find it puzzling that he was having trouble expressing himself. Garth reached out to caress her cheek, his gaze intent upon her face. "All I know is that I want you more than I've ever wanted anyone in my life, Elisa. I feel like I'll never get enough of you. I want it to be real between us—no more pretend-

167

ing, no more acting. I guess what I'm trying to say is that I want you to marry me."

Elisa's heart was drumming violently. "Marry you?" She could not speak beyond those two words. Loving him as she did, wasn't this what she had hoped and prayed to hear from Garth's lips?

Then the truth of it hit her like a douse of ice water in the face. Nothing had changed. Their relationship was still based on sexual attraction, at least on Garth's part. It was then Elisa discovered that wanting was not enough. She had to have it all. She needed for Garth to love her.

Her delicately marked brows drew together. "And what of love, Garth? You speak of wanting, of needing, but love has never once been mentioned." Elisa noted the quick frown he gave.

"I don't know if I even know what love is, honey," Garth stated with a faintly cynical smile. "From what I've seen the emotion is highly overrated and grossly unreliable."

"But a marriage based only on sexual desire . . . what chance would it have of working? What happens if the desire dies?" Elisa wondered aloud.

"It has as good a chance of working as any other reason," he stated in a rough tone. "There are more marriages that go on the rocks because the sex was never any good."

"Perhaps, but marriage is hard enough when two people love each other." Her voice was low and fervent. "I'm sorry, Garth, I can't marry you," she finally answered with forced calmness.

It was obvious he expected any answer but that. The man gripped her fingers so tightly, she winced. "I know that you want me as much as I want you, Elisa. Don't you think I can feel the way you tremble every time I take you into my arms? By the saints, woman, I could make love to you right now and you'd be begging for it!"

168

"Yes, I want you!" she cried out. "But that is not enough for me. Don't you understand?"

"You won't settle for anything less than a man's heart and soul, will you?" The contempt in his voice was hardly veiled.

Elisa felt she had to try to make him understand. She may not have his love, but she couldn't live with his hate. "Garth, don't you see it would never work for us? We'd end up hating each other."

"Don't patronize me, Elisa!" he hissed at her.

Something inside her snapped. "Dammit, man, you've made it abundantly clear that you don't want a working wife. Well, it just so happens that I've worked long and hard to get an education and I fully intend to put it to use." Elisa was warming up to her subject now. "You're so wrapped up in your work that you couldn't even find time to call me for three entire days. Why would that change once I was your wife? I won't marry a man who puts his career above his personal relationships." She was choking back the tears. "But most of all, I couldn't marry a man who doesn't love me." Elisa closed her eyes and shuddered. "It would never work, my—" She caught herself in time, the word "love" hovering on her tongue.

Garth finally broke in, his voice rich with anger. "You've got it all figured out, don't you, little girl?"

Elisa cringed at his reference. She was not a little girl, she wanted to shout; she was a woman.

The man was still speaking. "I've seen too many marriages torn apart, too many kids left to fend for themselves while both of their parents were out pursuing careers. A man has to provide for his family. He has no choice in the matter. A woman does. I work in a high-powered profession, Elisa, and I want my wife to be there when I get home from a tough day at the office."

"With pipe and slippers in hand, no doubt. Well, a lot

of women have to work, Garth, because they need the money to survive. They have families to provide for too."

"*My* wife would not need to work for the money."

"No, she wouldn't, but people do work for other reasons besides money." Elisa shot a quick sideways glance at him. "You're a wealthy man, aren't you?"

"Yes." He was neither coy nor a braggart about the fact.

"Could you live comfortably if you never worked another day in your life?"

"I suppose so," he admitted cautiously.

Elisa knew she had him. She had scored her point, but she did try not to gloat. "Then you work for reasons other than money, don't you?"

Garth simply looked at her in cool appraisal. Then he stood up and purposefully walked to the apartment door. Elisa suddenly realized he intended to walk out of her life as well, but she did not know what to say to stop him. He swung the door open and after a moment turned back to her.

"You know, you're right, Elisa. It never would work out for us. So long, sweetheart." The door closed quietly behind him.

Elisa realized later, with tears streaming down her face, that she had let Garth go without a word. Being right wasn't all it was cracked up to be, she decided rather belatedly. It was certainly no consolation for being alone. And Elisa was suddenly very much alone.

CHAPTER NINE

It was one of those balmy evenings in late September, marking the end of summer, the nip of approaching autumn in the air.

Elisa went through the familiar motions of locking the microfilm room and returning the key to its proper place. All part of the routine of closing up the library for the night.

"Hey, Connie," she called to the sprightly blonde working at the counter, "I know it's out of your way, but could I get a ride home with you after work? My car wouldn't start this morning," she added by way of explanation.

Elisa chose not to mention that she wouldn't have the money to get her car fixed until the end of the week. With the cost of her tuition for the fall term recently due, she found herself a little short of cash. Although Amanda and James had offered her financial assistance only the night before at dinner, she was still determined to make it on her own.

She hated to admit it, but some of her enthusiasm and unrelenting drive to complete her degree had mellowed. It was funny, but she actually seemed to be enjoying her studies more. She told herself it had nothing to do with Garth Brandau; after all, she had not seen the man for nearly two months. But in her heart Elisa knew she was not the same woman since his brief appearance in her life. She had both gained and lost something by loving him.

"Sure, I can give you a lift," said her co-worker after a moment's hesitation.

"I'd be glad to drive you home," cut in a serious, bespectacled young man named Joel, who worked in research. "I have to go in your direction anyway, Elisa."

"Oh, well, that's very kind of you, Joel, but . . ." Elisa started to make her excuses. Joel had asked her out several times in the past month, and she had turned him down on each occasion. It would be awkward to take advantage of his offer now. Most of the men she knew or met seemed somehow immature now. She supposed she had Garth Brandau to thank for that. Then Elisa looked at Connie and spied a hopeful light in her eyes.

"If you wouldn't mind, Elisa, I'm in kind of a hurry to get home. I have a late date with Greg tonight," the blond girl explained almost apologetically.

"Good heavens, you should have said so, Connie. Why don't you run along? I can finish up what little needs to be done here," suggested Elisa.

"If you're sure you don't mind . . ."

"Off you go this minute."

"Gee, thanks a million! I'll do the same for you sometime," said Connie, beaming.

"I have everything in my department wrapped up. We can go whenever you're ready," announced Joel rather gaily upon his return to Elisa's desk a few minutes later.

"I'll just get my things, then," she murmured, gathering up her sweater and pocketbook. "Are you sure you aren't going out of your way to run me home?" asked Elisa as they stepped out into the September night. "I thought you lived in the opposite direction."

172

"I do," the young man confessed sheepishly. "Ah, c'mon, Elisa, don't look at me like that. You wouldn't agree to go out with me, and taking you home is better than nothing. You can't blame me for trying."

"It's not you, Joel, honestly it isn't." They had stopped at the bottom of the grand stairway leading up to the library. "I haven't felt much like dating the past couple of months, that's all."

"I—I heard you went through a broken engagement this summer. I wasn't prying, really I wasn't. I don't even know where I heard it now. Oh, blast!" He dug his hands further into his pockets. "Look, Elisa, I—I—" He interrupted himself. "I say, there's a man over there watching us. Anyone you know?"

Without thinking, Elisa turned her head and peered into the dimly lit parking lot. She knew instinctively that the man leaning against the fancy white car was none other than Garth Brandau. If her eyes hadn't told her, her heart would have. She quickly looked back at Joel, confusion reigning in her mind. "Yes, I know who it is." Nothing could prevent the groan of despair that issued forth unbidden from her throat. "Damn!"

"Does that mean you'd prefer not to see him? Because whoever he is he's coming this way," her companion informed her. "I'll tell him to go away if that's what you want, Elisa." Joel slipped a protective arm around her waist.

"Thank you, that's really very sweet of you, but I'll handle this myself," she said with a weak smile. Joel tell Garth Brandau to beat it? Talk about the lamb roaring at the lion.

Long minutes seemed to tick away before the familiar drawl was heard directly behind her. "Hello, Elisa."

Bracing herself, she fixed a casual expression on her face and turned around. "H-hello, Garth." Her voice trembled

173

just a fraction. She disciplined her eyes to indifference, wanting to drink in the sight of him.

"I understand your car is out of commission. I'll give you a lift home. We can talk on the way," Garth stated, as if he expected her to come along without any fuss.

"Now wait just a minute . . ." sputtered Joel.

Elisa put out a hand to stop him, recognizing the dark scowl on the older man's face that clearly said "Who in the hell does this kid think he is?"

"It's all right," she said soothingly to the young man at her side who had gone pale by several shades. "This is an old friend of mine. Garth, this is Joel—" She started to make the proper introductions and drew a blank. "I'm sorry, Joel."

"It's Joel Burton," he said in a stilted voice, reluctantly offering his hand to the man.

"Garth Brandau—and I assure you I'm not trying to abduct Elisa. As a matter of fact, I'm her fiancé," he said, knowing full well it would disconcert her companion.

"Ex-fiancé," Elisa quickly corrected him.

"I'm sure it would only embarrass Mr. Burton to be made privy to our personal problems, darling." The man flashed her a warning. "We'll say good night now and be on our way." Garth nodded to the younger man as he took Elisa by the arm and drew her to his side.

"Elisa?" Joel looked at her, bewildered, as if she had somehow betrayed him.

She ought to tell Garth to go straight to hell, but she couldn't bring herself to do it. "I'm sorry, Joel. Thank you for the offer to drive me home."

"You had no right to tell Joel you were still my fiancé!" Elisa hissed at the man as they walked to his car. "You made me out to sound like a liar."

"I didn't like the way that young pup was hanging all over you in public like some damn infatuated teen-ager.

174

Good Lord, Elisa, I thought you had more sense than that! He has to be at least five years younger than you are."

"It's none of your damn business!" she spit out. It was maddening to be put on the defensive like that. She had never really thought about the difference in their ages, because she had not been interested in Joel. She had no intentions of informing Garth of that fact, however.

The next quarter of an hour was conducted in silence except for an impersonal "Thank you" and "You're welcome," exchanged when Garth settled her in the passenger's seat. He slipped behind the wheel of the Bentley and drove out of the parking lot, heading down a side street that more or less led in the direction of her apartment.

Elisa found the stifling atmosphere in the car anything but conducive to casual conversation. For a long time she simply stared out the window, although she had to confess later she had not seen a thing.

They were nearly to her street and still not another word had passed between them. Elisa didn't think she could stand much more of this. Garth had said he wanted to talk to her, yet nothing of the sort was happening.

The young woman self-consciously cleared her throat and said the first thing that came into her mind. "I hope the ring got back to you safely." She was careful to avoid mentioning the impersonal route she had chosen to assure its return, having hired a local security firm to perform the service.

"It was safely delivered. The necklace too." Garth's voice cut through the air like a blast of arctic wind. "Thanks for the note you enclosed with them."

Elisa ventured to lift her head for a moment. "B-but I didn't enclose a note."

"No, you didn't."

"Oh—" she broke off, surprised at the bitterness in his voice. There was no sense in trying to defend herself now. She had agonized about whether to send a note for days, had even drafted one a few dozen times, only to crumple up each effort in turn. In the end the package had been sent without one.

"How's school?" Garth finally inquired in a brisk tone.

Her chin snapped up. She was startled by the question. "Fine. How's everything going for you?"

"All right," Garth responded with a shrug. "How are Amanda and James? I haven't run into them since they got back from Europe."

"They're both fine," said Elisa, her voice emotionless.

"How did they take the news about our engagement being broken off?"

For the life of her Elisa couldn't figure out why he would bring up the subject of their engagement. She supposed she had started it by mentioning the ring, but she would have thought it was the last thing Garth would want to discuss.

"They were disappointed, naturally," she said, biting her lip.

"So was Helen, and you should have heard Sally and Jeff Cortland on the subject. They all liked you very much, Elisa."

"And I liked them," she said, showing a sudden interest in her hands.

"You know, it's funny," he said with a humorless laugh. "We used to have so much to say to one another. I sometimes thought we read each other's mind. Now it's like two strangers meeting for the first time."

Oh, never that, never as strangers, thought Elisa, but she did not voice the sentiment. She glanced up just as Garth pulled into a space in front of her apartment house. He turned off the car and sat there, hands frozen on the steering wheel, eyes straight ahead.

Then he turned to the woman beside him, his gaze curiously watchful, but the smile that slowly parted his lips decidedly sensual. It registered somewhere in the back

176

of Elisa's consciousness that the cashmere sweater Garth was wearing was the same shade of bewitching green as his eyes. It pulled taut across his chest, outlining the muscular perfection of the torso beneath as he slid an arm along the back of the seat. The man had certainly lost none of his attractiveness in the intervening months since their last meeting. It was not a thought to put Elisa's fears to rest.

Garth gently reached for her then and took her in his arms. "So, this is how it's going to end for us, little girl— one last kiss before I walk you to the door."

She was too stunned to pull away or even speak. After all the angry words, all the awkward, hackneyed phrases they had exchanged on the drive home, he was going to kiss her! Elisa didn't know whether to laugh or cry. Dear God, didn't the man know what it would do to her? To touch her very soul and then calmly walk out of her life again, surely this the last time. She would end up hating Garth as much as she loved him.

"No, Garth." Her voice sank almost to a whisper, unshed tears burning her eyes.

The man held her gaze a moment longer, then deliberately lowered his mouth to hers. It was intended to be a tender, gentle kiss, a last moment between lovers about to part, but somehow, as the man and woman touched, every carefully laid plan went up in smoke.

With a tortured groan Garth breathed the life back into her, setting her aflame, burning himself with the heat of the passion that raced through them like a forest fire sweeps a mountaintop.

Once the dam had been unleashed, there was no stopping the flood of desire that flowed back and forth between them. Mouth sought and found mouth, tongue teased tongue, as they drank long and sweet at the well of passion. Neither knew how long it was before they broke apart, each quickly retreating to a neutral corner.

"Well, we know now at least one thing hasn't changed

177

between us." Garth's laugh was ragged, and as quickly as it appeared, it vanished again, replaced by a thoughtful frown. "I can't really explain it, Elisa, but I had to see you tonight. I needed to hold you in my arms. I swear to God that's all I intended to do. I didn't mean for this to happen —not consciously anyway. But I'm not sorry it did."

"Neither am I," she echoed rather breathlessly.

The man entwined her fingers in his as though it were the only way he could trust himself not to touch her. "Listen, honey, we've got to talk. Is there anyone home at your place?"

"Yes," she moaned, "wouldn't you know it. Brenda isn't working tonight."

"Damn! Of course, she isn't. I talked to her myself earlier. That's how I found out your car had broken down." Garth ran a not-quite-steady hand through her mussed hair. "We'll just have to go to my place. All right? Because I definitely do not want an audience for what I have to say to you, Miss Harrington." He patted a spot on the seat beside him. "In the meanwhile scoot over here next to me."

After a moment's hesitation she did as he asked. Elisa curled up in the hollow of his arm, burrowing her face into the cashmere sweater, luxuriating in its softness, glorifying in her newfound freedom to actually touch him if she wished, and she did—as much to reassure herself it was really happening, that it wasn't all just a dream from which she would awaken, as anything. This was not the time to think, she told herself; it was only the time to feel.

The drive to Garth's apartment was made in record time. Once they were inside, the man leaned back against the door and slowly took Elisa into the circle of his arms. He seemed to savor the moment as a connoisseur would a fine wine. She knew he was going to kiss her and he did with such tenderness that it brought the tears to her eyes.

"Please, don't cry, darling. It's going to be all right, I

178

promise," he murmured, his words conveying the same message as his kiss. Elisa felt truly cherished for the first time in her life.

Then just when she was certain he was going to kiss her again, Garth pulled away. There was a scowl on his face as he stated in an entirely different tone, this one rather cool and detached, "I think we could both use a drink, don't you?"

Elisa wanted to shout at him that she didn't need a drink, that she only needed his arms around her as they had been only moments before, but something stopped her. "All right," she sighed wearily as she followed Garth into the living room.

She began to suspect something was wrong when she glanced up and saw Garth pouring straight Scotch into a rather large glass. Her impression of his drinking habits up until now had led her to believe he was a man of moderation. She was shocked, therefore, when he proceeded to down the liquor in a single gulp without even turning around.

"And what would *you* like to have?" he asked in a low, mocking tone.

"Whatever you're having is fine," she answered. It was of little or no consequence to her. She had no intentions of drinking what he gave her anyway. Something warned Elisa that she would need all of her wits about her in the next few minutes, unclouded by any alcohol. She watched as the man poured a second glass of amber liquid, this time adding a measure of water and several ice cubes.

"Why don't you sit down, Elisa, and make yourself at home?" he suggested, handing her the drink. "You look like a scared little rabbit standing there. You have my word I'm not about to pounce on you." Garth's mood seemed to have taken a turn for the worse.

"I never thought you were," she said, mumbling, not very subtly masking her irritation.

Garth retraced his steps to the bar and fixed himself what appeared to Elisa to be another double Scotch. Then he turned around and faced her, but remained where he was, making no move to come any closer. As the minutes ticked by, the scenario still did not alter.

"Look, Garth," she ventured at last, having had it up to there with the man. "You said we were coming back here to talk. Well, it seems to me there has been a whole lot of drinking and very little talking so far. And you're acting funny too. I don't like it one bit."

He thrust his head forward suddenly. "What's the matter, sweetheart? Haven't you ever seen a man trying to work up his courage before? You're supposed to be the psychologist—how would you diagnose it?" he added with sarcasm.

Elisa sucked in her breath. The possibility that Garth might feel unsure of himself had never occurred to her. "Oh, Garth, I—"

"No, let me finish. You know what they say: 'The bigger they are, the harder they fall.'"

She smiled in spite of herself, thinking back to that afternoon so many months before when Charlotte had said the same thing to her. For once in her life Charlotte had been right.

"And well you might laugh," Garth grated through his teeth, "because you are about to witness one of the biggest take a nosedive!" He broke off abruptly and gave his full attention to the glass of Scotch in his hand.

"I—I wasn't laughing!" she hotly defended herself. "I was smiling because someone once said that would happen to me."

"I lied to you, Elisa," he went on as if he hadn't heard her. "When you asked me how everything was going and I said all right, I was lying. Nothing has been right for weeks. None of it seems to mean a damn thing to me anymore."

"Garth, I'm sorry." But she didn't sound as sorry as she should have somehow. In fact, she sounded almost hopeful.

"You know, honey, I'd always thought of myself as a man who didn't really need other people. If it makes you feel any better, I've found out that there's at least one person in this world I do need. When I walked out of your apartment that night, I told myself it wasn't any different than the other times I'd walked out on a woman. What a damnable fool I was!"

"We've all been a fool at one time or another, Garth. We're all human."

"Yeah, well, I discovered just how human I am. My job, the house in the country, even the money I've always had—none of it matters, nothing does without you. That's what the last nine weeks have shown me. God, sometimes it seems like nine years!" He finished off the drink and reached for a refill.

"Oh, Garth, no—don't!" Elisa got to her feet and crossed the room to stand beside him.

"Pity, Elisa? Now, that is rich." His gaze seemed to strip the cotton blouse and skirt from her.

"You silly man, don't you understand anything?" She shook his arm. "After the night you went away, I think I understood for the first time why someone would drink to forget. But I didn't. I loved you so much that I even cherished the pain that came with it. The pain was all I had left. It was the only thing that proved I was still alive. I love you, Garth. I've been in love with you since that day out by Spring Green. You aren't the only one who has lived through a lifetime in the past two months." Her voice was raised in anger and anguish.

"I'm not very good at expressing my feelings, Elisa," he said with a strange air of speaking at random. "I haven't had much practice at it."

"We're two mature adults, Garth. For God's sakes, no

more pretense, no more games or carefully worded phrases. We have to be honest with each other now. What are you trying so hard to say to me?" she groaned.

"I haven't said this to anyone since I was almost too young to remember and then it was to my mother—but I love you, honey. I think I've been falling in love with you since the night you offered me a chicken salad sandwich and a glass of milk. I just didn't know what it was at the time." The mask he had always held in place, even when they were alone, was finally lowered. Elisa saw there in his eyes what she had hoped and prayed for—love, bright and unfettered. Here, then, was the man who had conceived the Spring Green house.

"I love you and you love me. What could be simpler or more wonderful than that?" Elisa laughed through her tears. She put her arms around the man's waist and snuggled up as close as she possibly could. "Enough talking, Garth Brandau. We have nine weeks and three days to make up for."

"Not yet, we don't. I love you more than I'll ever be able to tell you, Elisa." He kissed both of her eyelids and the tip of her shiny nose. "And if I start to make love to you now, I'll never get said what I have to say—so behave yourself, at least for the time being," he chuckled, slapping at the hand trying to snake its way under his sweater.

"Oh, all right," she pouted.

"I want us to be together, honey. I want you for my wife. We can work it out, I know we can. I'll give you the money to finish graduate school—"

The young woman was already shaking her head no.

"All right, I'll *loan* you the money to finish, but I get to set the terms for repayment," said Garth with intense satisfaction.

"You drive a hard bargain, Mr. Brandau," she teased, "but I accept."

"We'll buy a house here in town and Ophelia can come

live with us. I promise she won't be banished to the back porch either."

"Can we really buy a house?" Her voice raised half an octave.

"Of course, didn't I just say so, I'm a wealthy man, honey, or had you forgotten? Once we have children, we'll work out a way for me to work at home part of the time so you can continue with your career too. Other couples have done it. We can too."

Elisa looked up at the man, her eyes round as saucers. "I—I can't take it all in, Garth. You're going too fast for me. I thought you didn't want your wife to have a career?"

"I just don't want us to end up like my parents, Elisa. I think I finally understand why my mother had to leave and I don't want to ever lose you for the same reason. It will work, honey. We're good together. We may sometimes bite and scratch like a couple of alley cats, but in the end love will win out because we're only half alive without each other."

"Are you quite finished now, darling, because I would very much like to kiss you?" She drew the last word along the line of his bottom lip with her fingernail.

"Not quite." Garth released her and disappeared into his study.

"Now what the—" she grumbled, but her eyes were dancing. "I never thought I'd say this, Garth Brandau," she shouted at the top of her lungs so he would be sure to hear every word in the next room, "but sometimes *you* talk too much!"

Then he reappeared, at first looking no different from when he had left. Garth walked straight up to Elisa and kissed her long and hard on the mouth. "Elisa Harrington, will you marry me?"

She nearly burst out laughing, but stifled the urge at the sight of his serious face. "Yes, I will marry you," she pronounced with all the solemnity due such an occasion.

183

"In that case," he grinned, "I believe I have something that belongs to you."

Garth produced a jewelry case from behind his back and flipped open the lid. There, side-by-side, were her diamond engagement ring and the heart pendant he had given her the night of her twenty-fifth birthday.

"It looks like a perfect fit," he smiled, slipping the ring onto her finger. "Now if you'll just turn around, darling, I'll be happy to do the honors," instructed Garth, draping the necklace about her throat.

An inadvertent shiver ran through her as the cold metal touched her skin. But ice was quickly followed by fire as a pair of warm lips found the sensitive hollow just below her ear. Elisa's breath caught in her throat. Garth's mouth was mapping out each bone of her neck and shoulders. He impatiently pushed her blouse to one side, unveiling new territories to his exploration. This time when she began to quiver all over, it was for a far better reason.

Elisa turned and found herself in Garth's embrace as she had dreamed of so often. The words of love, once so difficult for him to say, flowed freely from his lips. The physical side of their relationship had always burned like white-hot embers in promise. Now, fanned by their mutual discovery of love and banked by a commitment made to each other from the depth of their souls, it burst into an all-consuming flame.

Garth's muscular hands in turn massaged and caressed her back and hips. Elisa pressed ever closer to him, loving the feel of his sinewy form against her, wanting more when she discovered that the intimacy only intensified the aching need inside her.

She moved her own hands down the front of his cashmere sweater until she found the expanse of bare skin where the sweater had pulled away from his slacks. She ran her palms up under it, her fingers eagerly reacquainting themselves with the riot of soft hair and the hard contours of his chest and abdomen.

"Dear God, Elisa, I can't take much more of this," he muttered with a thick tongue as his mouth released hers.

The young woman's eyes burned like dark coals. "I love you, Garth. I want you to love me."

"I do. With every breath that I take I worship you."

"Then love me as a man loves a woman. Show me the way, my darling."

"We can be married this week by special license, Elisa. Are you sure?"

"Please don't make me spend even one more night without your arms around me. Garth. I need you now," she whispered, standing on tiptoe to wrap her arms around his neck. "You turned out to be the damnedest man to seduce," she murmured enticingly in his ear.

With a low husky chuckle Garth swept her up in his arms and carried her down the hallway to his bedroom. He gently put Elisa on the bed and lay down beside her. Then he began to kiss her, to caress her, to show her all the many ways of love. His hands moved under her to mold her thighs to his, making her all the more aware that his need was as great as her own.

The buttons of her blouse were deftly undone, leaving a long length of golden skin visible. The single hook between her breasts was released, the lacy covering falling away to reveal the twin mounds beneath, their tips pink and hard in the throes of the passion he aroused in her. Sensual fingers slowly encircled the darkened peaks. With one breast molded in his hand, the other was supped at by his hungry mouth.

Then Garth suddenly pulled away, leaving her there on the bed cold and bereft without the warmth of his body. Elisa knew one moment of despair before the realization came that he was not leaving her altogether. He pulled the sweater over his head and quickly dispensed with the rest

185

of their clothing. When his body was once again eased down on top of hers, the last encumbrance between them was gone.

Their hands and lips eagerly explored all the secret intimate places a man and woman were meant to discover together. Then Garth's mouth sought hers once more, his tongue parting her eager, willing lips as his legs came between hers.

The frenzied passion of their union caught them up in its primal force, and all else was forgotten but the wild, sweet joining of their bodies in love. Each murmured the other's name a thousand times, whispering in the night all the words in their hearts as they showed each other the way love should be for a man and a woman.

Later, as the two of them lay laughing and talking in the afterglow of their love, Garth whispered near her ear.

"Brenda won't be worried when you don't come in tonight, will she?"

She drowsily curled up closer to him, drawn by his warmth. "No, she won't miss me until morning. I'll call her first thing."

The man's kiss trailed across her bare shoulders, setting her aquiver all over again, his pleasure made tenfold by her immediate response to his touch. "First thing?" he laughed.

She turned to him and saw the fire rekindled in his eyes. "Well . . . second anyway."

When You Want A Little More Than Romance–

Try A Candlelight Ecstasy!

The unforgettable saga of a magnificent family

IN JOY AND IN SORROW

by JOAN JOSEPH

They were the wealthiest Jewish family in Portugal, masters of
Europe's largest shipping empire. Forced to flee the scourge of
the Inquisition that reduced their proud heritage to ashes, they
crossed the ocean in a perilous voyage. Led by a courageous,
beautiful woman, they would defy fate to seize a forbidden
dream of love.

A Dell Book   **$3.50**   **(14367-5)**

The second volume in the spectacular Heiress series

The Cornish Heiress

by Roberta Gellis
bestselling author of
The English Heiress

Meg Devoran—by night the flame-haired smuggler, Red Meg.
Hunted and lusted after by many, she was loved by one man
alone...

Philip St. Eyre—his hunger for adventure led him on a
desperate mission into the heart of Napoleon's France.

From midnight trysts in secret smugglers' caves to wild
abandon in enemy lands, they pursued their entwined destinies
to the end—seizing ecstasy, unforgettable adventure—and
love.

A Dell Book $3.50   (11515-9)

Danielle

**AMERICA'S
LEADING
LADY OF
ROMANCE
REIGNS
OVER ANOTHER BESTSELLER**

A Perfect Stranger

A flawless mix of glamour and love by
Danielle Steel, the bestselling author of
The Ring, Palomino and *Loving.*

A DELL BOOK $3.50 #17221-7

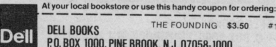

Dell Bestsellers